HILL SCHOO
ROAD, S.E.2

DRUMMOND HILL CREW
LIVIN' LARGE
When a show-off comes on the scene... There has to be TROUBLE!
YiNkA AdEbAyO
X

path after her and jumped into the back of the car. Yvonne started the car and drove off.

"Anyway, I don't see what all the fuss is about. I mean, after all, netball is only a poor excuse for a game," Darren stated with the air of a young Einstein. "Now, basketball — that's a serious game."

The boys were playing a game of knuckles. Darren leaned back in the seat caressing his hand. He'd had his knuckles rapped hard and they were throbbing. And it was Tyrone's turn again. "I don't think we should carry on," Darren said, staring absently out of the window as the scenery flashed past.

"Aw!" complained Tyrone. "And I was starting to enjoy myself."

"Nah, there's no point. There's not enough room in the car to play it properly," Darren said, waving his arms around. "Then there's Mum swinging the car around from side to side so I keep missing."

Tyrone kissed his teeth. He knew a feeble excuse when he heard it. He leaned back in the seat. It was always the same when he and Darren played any games. Darren would want to carry on with a game if he was winning, but it was a different matter if things weren't going his way.

"Anyway," Darren continued, "I'm getting bored." He nodded his head nonchalantly in time to the music on the car radio.

Tyrone closed his eyes. There was no point in arguing. Darren would only start railing up.

"I wonder if the girls are going to make it to the canal next week?" Darren inquired suddenly, nudging Tyrone in the ribs.

Tyrone shrugged his shoulders. "Who can say? You know how Remi and Tenisha are."

Darren nodded in agreement. Tyrone was right. Remi Oluseyi and Tenisha Markham were two Drummond Hill Comprehensive girls with whom they often hung around. They were typical girls as far as the boys were concerned; they'd say one thing when all the time they meant something else.

"If they don't want to come we'll just go without them," Darren said. Then, changing the subject, he added, "I really want that new leather jacket I saw advertised in the magazine."

"Yeah, Remi bought an identical one, you'll both look cool when you come to the Youth Club," Tyrone said, patting down his high-top hairstyle.

Darren craned his neck to admire his reflection in the rearview mirror of the car. He agreed that the jacket would definitely look good on him. "I'm not really into wearing the same style of garms as other kids... but Remi does have an idea when it comes to fashion. So I guess it's okay." Darren patted down his high-top hairstyle as well.

He and Tyrone didn't care much for the cuts that most of the other boys were into. None of those cuts with logos and dollar signs for them. No, they always cut their hair the same way and always used the same barber. No other barber was allowed even to think about cutting their hair.

As far as Darren and Tyrone were concerned, no one else in their year at Drummond Hill knew how to dress. They were all totally uncool. "It's all about style," Darren liked to boast. "And we've got tons of it." Tyrone always agreed.

"Here we are," declared Yvonne, parking the car outside the leisure centre.

Darren breathed an audible sigh of relief as he jumped out of the car. The three of them made their way towards the crowd which had gathered by the netball court. There was quite a turnout. Yvonne was pleased and relieved when she spotted her husband chatting amiably to other parents.

With a blast of the referee's whistle, the final match was under way. The players quickly got into their stride and both teams scored early. It was a hectic end-to-end game with both teams playing exceptionally well to a chorus of approving cheers and disapproving jeers from their respective supporters, but the look on the faces of Patricia and the rest of the Drummond Hill team was of sheer determination in refusing to allow the visitors to get away with a victory.

However well his sister played, Darren remained unconvinced about the validity of a netball game. He nudged Tyrone suddenly and shouted in his friend's ear above the din. "Look, that's what I mean," he said, pointing. "Netball is such a silly game, you aren't even allowed to bounce the ball. How can you show skill if you can't dribble the ball?"

"But you wouldn't expect them to bounce it," said Tyrone, instantly warming to the discussion, "it's got a completely different set of rules."

"That doesn't mean anything. Rules are there to be broken. If it was left to me I'd invent a new set of rules. I'd allow the ball to be bounced; if you want to try a jump shot — go ahead."

Darren was still complaining when Patricia intercepted a ball in the semi-circle, swivelled her hips expertly and threw the ball into the net. At this point, Darren's parents jumped up, waving and cheering loudly.

"Even you've got to admit, that was a bit special," Tyrone remarked.

"Fluke, that's what it was," Darren scoffed. "Look, I've had enough of this netball rubbish. Let's go to the games room and see whose cash we can take on the machines. There's always some fool waiting to bet money that he can beat me."

"Patricia won't be pleased if you leave before the end of the match."

"Good," said Darren. "Then she'll know what it feels like not to get your own way all the time."

Still, Tyrone thought they should let Yvonne know where they were going. "Will it be okay if we go and have a look at the games machines, Mrs James?" he asked.

Darren raised his eyes to the ceiling. Sometimes Tyrone could be just a bit too goody-goody.

"What?" Yvonne said, breathlessly. "What games? Where?" She turned suddenly back to the netball court, where Patricia had got possession of the ball again and was aiming to shoot at the goal. "Come on Patricia!" she shouted, at which moment Patricia threw the ball towards the net — and missed. She shot her mother a withering look, so Yvonne would be in no doubt that she'd shouted at just the wrong moment.

Darren tugged at Yvonne's sleeve and pointed to the far end of the sports hall. "The games machines are through that door, Mum. We're going, okay?"

"Oh, all right then." Yvonne waved them away. "Just keep an eye on the match and come back when it's over..."

But the boys didn't hear. They were already scooting over towards the games room that was full of bleeping machines.

The two friends shoved and nudged each other playfully in the ribs as they struggled for the first play, but in the end Tyrone stepped back as Darren shoved his coins into the machine. The screen cleared and the game spluttered into life.

Darren had just begun the game when Tyrone's attention was diverted by a boy craning his neck over Darren's shoulder. It was someone he'd never seen before. The boy was about the same age as Darren and Tyrone, though he was smaller than they. His head was shaved at the sides, with small funky dreads on the top, and he wore the kind of clothes and had the kind of attitude that made Tyrone nod his head in approval.

"How 'bout I play you?" the boy said to the back of Darren's head. "Just for a laugh, though," he added. "You wouldn't want to play me seriously, man, because I'm the best. You couldn't beat me."

Tyrone grinned broadly. This was the challenge he and Darren had been waiting for. The new boy had seen some of Darren's game, but he didn't know what Darren could really do with the machine — and that was the whole point. This was their hustle. Darren had made it look like he wasn't so good at Street Fighter to try and attract a sucker like this. Now they would get him to play for money and they would be rich by the end of the evening.

Darren looked round from his game. "You biggin' yourself up, bwoy," he said to the kid with dreads. "I'm the best here, always have been. I got no reason to play you."

"Not unless you make it interesting... you know, worth his while to play," Tyrone quipped.

"Shall we say fifty pence a game?" Darren added, and he grinned slyly at Tyrone.

"Sure," said the other boy. "But you better have a lot of cash on you, because you're gonna lose it."

"If you say so, bwoy," said Darren knowingly.

"I'm not your 'bwoy'." The new boy sounded suddenly threatening. "Call me Junior, or call me nothing."

Junior slapped down a fifty-pence piece on the side of the Street Fighter machine and Darren did the same. He and Tyrone were at bursting point. They stifled giggles and only just managed to restrain themselves from falling about with laughter as they imagined what they would spend their winnings on. Darren was thinking how lucky he was to have found someone who was going to contribute towards the price of the new jacket he wanted. Feeling pleased with himself, he pulled the hood of his puffa over his head and whistled a tune from the new CD he'd recently bought. He was confident because, when it came to computer games, he was known as the Drummond Hill Hotstepper.

Darren stepped up to the machine and selected Ryu, his favourite character. He worked the buttons gracefully, knowing that Junior didn't stand a chance.

But Junior had other ideas. He, too, was experienced at playing Street Fighter, and from the moment he saw Darren and Tyrone at the machine he'd known that they were trying to hustle someone into losing their money. He had known this because he was a hustler too. He was a hustler who had hustled Darren and Tyrone into thinking they could win. He had hustled the hustlers.

Again and again, Junior's character kicked at Ryu, and it wasn't long before Darren sensed he was in trouble. His fingers worked harder and faster and he began to kick his legs against the machine with the effort of it all. But it was clear to him — and to Tyrone, who stood anxiously by — that Ryu was going down.

This is not how it was meant to be.

Suddenly, Yvonne was behind them. "C'mon you guys, the match is over. We've been waiting for you."

Darren sighed, pretending to sound annoyed as he stepped away from the unfinished game. "You got lucky, I guess," he said to Junior.

"Yeah, right." Junior, raised an eyebrow. "And I'm the Queen of Sheba."

"I said, you got lucky," Darren said through clenched teeth. "And I know what I'm talking about."

Junior kissed his teeth as he turned his back and walked away, deftly picking up Darren's fifty pence as he went. Darren was so shocked by the new boy's cheek that all he could do was stand there with his mouth open.

It was Tyrone who offered Darren a way to save face. "Your mum rescued that guy from a fate worse than death," he said, trying to sound confident.

"Too right. I hadn't even got my game flowing properly. He wouldn't have known what hit him."

Throughout the journey home Darren sat quietly and stared out of the window of the car. Dad was now driving as mum's feet were hurting from wearing those high-heeled shoes.

"Patricia played really well. Don't you think so, Darren?" Yvonne asked.

Darren didn't respond, so Lester spoke for him. "First class!"

"And she scored the winning points," Yvonne added.

Patricia beamed proudly at her brother and whispered, "Wicked!"

Darren's mood grew even darker. He wished that the journey would end so he could show Tyrone how skilful he was at basketball instead.

CHAPTER TWO

The playground of Drummond Hill Comprehensive was already teeming with pupils when Darren and Tyrone strolled through the gates the following morning. As usual, the two friends made their way across the basketball courts towards the bike sheds.

"Can't you see we've got a game on here?" whined a grubby Year 7 boy who had been engaged in a one-on-one basketball duel with a friend. Darren stared at him menacingly for a moment and then cuffed him with the back of his hand. The boy let out a yelp of pain. He was just about to start cussing but something in the way Darren looked at him made him think otherwise, and he simply walked away, nursing his throbbing head. Tyrone could not be sure, but he thought he heard the boy kiss his teeth as Darren picked up his ball and bounced it a couple of times.

"Stupid Year 7 kids think they can come up and distress the scene," Darren said importantly. That was the thing with Year 7 kids, they only gave you respect if you treated them rough.

Darren gave the young boy another dismissive stare as he readied himself for a try at three points. He fixed his eyes on the target and bent his knees. Bringing the ball to head height, he jumped straight off the ground and delivered the shot at the top of his jump, flicking his wrist on the follow-through. The ball bounced off the back board, danced around the rim, then dropped down through the net.

"Well wicked," Tyrone complimented as they both flicked their fingers and left the basketball court, making their way over to the bike sheds.

Anton, Remi and Tenisha were already

there. Tenisha was jawing away, spinning another of her tall stories. Anton was rolling his eyes upwards in disbelief when Tyrone and Darren arrived.

Tenisha blinked owlishly through the spectacles that she wore on the end of her nose. She removed them and looked thoughtfully at everybody, the way she always did when she was going to say something important.

"I thought I was going to die," she declared.

"Why's that?" Darren enquired as he, Anton and Tyrone touched fists in greeting.

Tenisha squinted, all the while fingering the piece of Elastoplast that held the frame of her glasses together, before resuming her tale.

"When I went to the swimming baths with my dad," she said, satisfying herself that her glasses were clean enough, then replacing them, precariously, on the end of her nose.

"I can imagine," Darren scoffed. "Doing the backstroke, beer gut sticking upwards, he must have looked as if he was pregnant.

Shame, man! I'd rather be buried up to my neck with sand and have a million ants thrown over me."

Tenisha continued. "That would have been bad enough. But I saw this boy I fancy. And just as he noticed me for the first time all afternoon, Dad got an urge to dive off the top board..." Tenisha was now visibly cringing. "So there he was, his tummy hanging over his trunks, and he belly-flopped into the pool. Then — this is when it gets really horrible — just as he hits the water, his trunks come off! Can you imagine? I could have died with shame!"

Tyrone was laughing so hard he almost fell over. Good old Tenisha, she always managed to come out with stories that would keep them chuckling for ages, though it was usually because the stories were so obviously big fat lies.

"Anyway, this drop-dead gorgeous boy, who'd been giving me the eye all afternoon, I might add," Tenisha continued, "realises that it's my dad that's splashing around like a distressed turtle and he starts laughing."

"That must have been awful," Remi said, placing a comforting arm around Tenisha's shoulder.

"Yeah, it was. The boy was laughing so much I thought he was going to pee himself."

"It's obvious from the way he was acting that he wasn't worth it. Count yourself lucky that he didn't ask you out."

Tenisha turned to face Remi. "It's easy for you to say that — you always have a posse of boys offering to carry your books for you or offering to pay your bus fare in the mornings. I should be so lucky!"

"Yeah, but have you seen the state of them? Most are real saddos."

"I wouldn't even mind that," Tenisha sniffed, shrugging her shoulders. "I'm avoided as though I had the plague."

"You think I'm lucky? That's because you haven't seen them. One boy was even refused a part as an extra in the film *It Came From Outer Space*."

Darren thought this was particularly funny, and he was still laughing when

Tyrone nudged him in the ribs. "I think you've got a customer," he said.

"Hey, Darren."

It was Nipper, the shortest boy in their year.

"What's up?" Darren asked, wiping a tear from his eye."Let me guess, you want a loan."

"How did you know?"

"What other reason would you need to come and distress the scene. How much?"

"A pound."

Darren screwed his face up. "Mmm, I think I can manage that. Same rates?"

"Yeah, I know — fifteen per cent by tomorrow lunchtime."

"What's that, Ty?" Darren asked his friend, fishing out a few coins from his pocket.

"Fifteen pence interest. I'll write it in the book."

While Tyrone searched furtively inside his school bag for his notebook and pencil, Darren dropped the coins into the outstretched hand in front.

The two girls, who had been standing to one side while the transaction was taking place, turned to face each other. Remi spoke, full of admiration and respect. "You have to big up Darren for the way he deals with business."

Tenisha nodded in agreement.

Suddenly the bell sounded to signal the beginning of school. At the same time Darren decided that he needed to use the loo. By the time he had finished and stumbled into class, Mr Robertson had already started the lesson.

"What time do you call this?" spluttered the teacher, holding his wrist out in such a way that Darren could see the second hand of his watch ticking.

Darren shrugged. He knew that it was hopeless to argue with teachers when they were in one of these moods. So he simply made his way along the rows of desks and chairs.

Mr Robertson continued: "I shall have to put you on report, James."

Darren groaned inwardly without looking backwards. It was like that on some days.

He'd come to school pleased with life and then one of the teachers would go and spoil it by picking on him for no reason whatsoever. He found his seat at the back and scowled angrily through the rest of the lesson.

Mr Robertson kept his promise and put Darren on report. This wouldn't have been so bad, but he also called Darren's mother to let her know what had happened. Even that might not have have been so disastrous for Darren, if his mother had not put his dad in such a dark mood. If she hadn't kept on about the grey hairs that had started to sprout up all over his head, things would have been relatively safe.

"It's not so bad, Lester. It gives you a more mature look," Yvonne had said.

"Do you mean I look old?"

She had laughed at him and tried to soothe him by telling him how she really liked it, and how grey hair was a sign of distinction and experience.

"If that's the case, why do all the young kids start offering me their seats on the bus?"

Yvonne made it worse by laughing and saying that they did it out of respect.

Lester said nothing in response. He ran a hand through his greying hair. Pushing his chair backwards, he got up and walked briskly over to the living room, flicking through the TV channels with the remote control before making himself comfortable in the large armchair.

Darren did not know whether his mum was right or not, but he did know that when Dad was in one of those moods it was best to keep well away from him. But today he knew he couldn't leave it alone. He still needed some money to buy that jacket he had promised himself, and so he decided to try and sweet talk it out of his dad.

"Dad! Do you want a game on my computer?"

Darren knew that his pops was like him — he couldn't resist a challenge. Soon they would be upstairs sitting cross-legged on the floor of his bedroom, twiddling and toggling away with the computer console. A wry smile spread across Darren's face.

But Mr James didn't look up; he stared blankly at the flickering set.

Darren decided to ask again. He couldn't be certain that his dad had heard him the first time. "Dad, I've got this wicked racing game," he said.

Mr James's reaction was not the one that his son had been expecting. He raised his hand and waved Darren away.

Sometimes it was not that easy to get his dad to do things. There was only one person in the James household that had those skills: Patricia, Darren's older sister. She could get anything from her father. A shy flutter of her eyes and he'd be searching furtively in his pockets, shoving fistfuls of fivers under her nose as though money was going out of fashion.

Darren hated Patricia. What annoyed him most was that he knew his method of getting money from his dad came a distant second to hers. She had the easiest, no-nonsense, works-every-time-without-fail plan. When she did it, Darren could do nothing but watch, his mouth open with admiration.

You could always tell when Patricia was readying herself to ask. She would wait until Dad had settled himself in front of the TV for the evening. Then, sliding up beside him with a doe-like expression in her eyes, she'd give him a big hug.

Yeuck! Darren could never do that, though Dad didn't seem to be able to resist it.

Patricia would follow that with the hound-dog look, and quicker than you could say "lipstick counter at the chemist" — which was always the first place that she would make for when she got the money — Dad would dig his fist deep into his pocket, slipping out crisp notes.

"But Dad, you'll love this game, it's the new 3D simulator," said Darren hopefully.

Mr James sat motionless. "I've been talking to your mother," he said at last.

Darren groaned inwardly. What had he done now? His mind raced as he tried hard to recall what had gone on that day.

"Yes, your mother tells me that she's been getting disturbing reports about your behaviour at school. What have you got to say for yourself?"

What did he want him to say? "I'm sorry and I won't do it again?" "The teachers keep picking on me?" He had used all those excuses and he knew that they would not work this time. Darren shrugged his shoulders in resignation; it was best to take it on the chin.

But this attitude seemed to infuriate his father further. "If you don't pull your socks up, young lad, we will have to seriously consider sending you to another school," he said. "That's if we can find one to take you in."

With that, his dad dismissed him.

CHAPTER THREE

The following morning things started badly for Darren. He was making his way towards the bathroom when Patricia charged out of her bedroom and slipped in before him, locking the door behind her.

"Open up," Darren shouted as he banged on the door with his fists. "I was here first."

Patricia didn't answer. Darren could hear her running the taps and singing loudly at the top of her voice.

His sister was always getting her own way. Darren had lost count of the times he'd heard the boys at Drummond Hill Comprehensive saying how gorgeous she was. Patricia was very athletic and lithe, with a pixie face which belied her determined nature. When Darren heard his sister described as 'gorgeous', he would stagger around the playground as though he had been shot, holding his neck with his hands and making as if he was being sick.

The older boys, who would otherwise give him a hard kick in the pants as they usually did with all the kids in Year 7 and 8, would beckon Darren over with a crooked finger and invite him to sit with them. Darren, smiling, would strut over, taking care that Tyrone and the rest could see. He'd open his hand gladly as the Year 10 boys would offer him some sweets. If he was lucky they'd even hand him a few football stickers or some loose change.

"Put in a good word for me!" they'd plead as they wrapped a friendly arm around his shoulders.

Darren would be up for it, and he'd carry out his part of the bargain. It wasn't his fault if Patricia turned up her nose and shouted at the top of her voice, "No way, he's butters," or, "He's got a peanut-shaped head." It wasn't his fault if she had her eye on someone else. He'd take the sweets anyway.

"That's the thing with having an elder sister," Darren would say to Tyrone as they ate the goodies and kept the treats, "they come in handy when you're a bit stuck for cash."

He wasn't thinking that this morning as he stood on the landing shivering in his slippers. All he was thinking about was not being late for school. If he was late again, he'd really be in for it.

"She must be late again," said Mr James, suddenly interrupting Darren's train of thought. He was talking to no one in particular, making his way down to the dining room. Darren knew his dad would have behaved differently if it was him who had rushed into the bathroom like that.

His gaze fell and he stared at the flowered pattern on the wallpaper. "Yeah, well I'm late too, or hadn't you noticed?" he said quietly under his breath.

"How many times have I told you two..." Mr James rambled on, shaking his head. "Set your clock half an hour earlier!"

Darren nodded respectfully and waited outside the bathroom door, hopping around impatiently.

"I had better get ready myself, or else I'll be late," Dad mused absently.

After what seemed like an eternity to Darren, Patricia finally emerged from the bathroom. He went in, scowling at her, then locked the door behind him.

Holding his toothbrush, he squeezed a dollop of paste on to it, then slapped his hand to his forehead as a thought struck him. "Mr Singh's detention class!" he cried to himself. Why had this stupid netball-playing sister held him up? Today of all days! After school today there was basketball practice, when Mr Adams would be picking the team. There was no way Mr Singh would let you off from one of his after-school punishment classes. He was one of those teachers that all the kids were frightened of displeasing.

Today of all days he had to get to school on time.

The pupils at Drummond Hill all believed that the turban Mr Singh wore each day had hidden meanings. Some kids said that you could tell what mood he was in by the colour of the material he chose to wrap his head in. They had made up this rhyme:

If Mr Singh's wearing blue, use the loo,
If he's wearing green, try not to be seen,
And if his turban's red, 'nuff said.

Darren had once asked Mr Singh why he wore the turban. Mr Singh had replied that the word came from a Persian word, *Dulband*, which means 'scarf' around the head. It didn't really answer the question, but Darren could check for that — after all, he and his bredrin wore baseball caps.

Back in his room Darren searched for his school bag. "Whew!" he exclaimed. "Lucky I packed everything last night."

He skipped down the stairs two at a time and rushed out of the door, shouting goodbye to anyone who was listening.

Darren's school bag felt heavier this

morning, on account of the maths lesson he had that afternoon. One thing that struck Darren about maths text books was how heavy they were. Everyone in his class was always going on about this. Darren wished that he didn't have maths today — the strap of his bag was digging into his shoulder and he found that he couldn't run very fast. On any other day he would have sprinted down Acacia Avenue, but this morning he found the best he could manage was a slow jog. It was as if everything was against him; even the road seemed longer this morning. He was breathing heavily, taking deep gulps of air and willing his legs to move a little faster.

By the time he reached the corner of Wood Lane and the High Street there were large drops of sweat on his brow. He squinted as he tried to make out whether the right bus was coming. He flicked a tongue out as a trickle of sweat rolled slowly down his face. It tasted salty. Wiping his brow with the back of his hand, he increased his pace when he saw the bus. As he ran for it, knowing he would catch it, Darren felt relieved that he would make it to school on time — just. He would not have to endure the torture of Mr Singh's after-school club.

After showing his bus pass to the driver, Darren slumped into a seat near the front of the top deck and stared absent-mindedly out of the window, daydreaming about the forthcoming basketball match.

Darren prided himself on his dribbling and shooting skills for the school team; he had won the previous match almost single-handedly. His mind raced as he remembered how he had been given the task of taking two free shots from the free throw line. There were only seconds remaining in the match, and Drummond Hill Comprehensive needed both points to win. Standing in front of the basket he'd reminded himself that he'd been faced with similar throws in practice. But as he stood there, listening to the opposing players trying to put him off with cries of, "I bet you a fiver you miss," and, "Remember to bend your knees," butterflies had started in his stomach. Composing himself, he had thrown the ball, as he had been taught, successfully into the middle of the basket. The second throw was identical to the first.

With a shout of joy Mr Adams, the sports teacher, had run on to the playing area, grabbed Darren by the waist and carried him over his head to the side of the court.

With rising excitement, Darren now thought of what he would do to the next team they faced. It would all be so simple if Tyrone and the rest of the team passed to him whenever they had the ball. All they had to do was give it to him and leave the rest to him. He wondered why the rest even bothered to turn up. After all, it wasn't as though they did a lot, was it? He was the star of the team.

Darren's mind was still on the game he had won as the bus stopped violently, throwing him forward in his seat. His head jerked backwards as he braced himself with his hands on the seat in front. From the back of the bus he heard a cry. Someone had banged their forehead on one of the metal posts.

"Bwooy!" Darren exclaimed when peeped out of the window to see what had caused the bus to brake so hard. He slapped his hand to his head in frustration. This could not be happening. Darren could see a man with a checked flat cap standing in the middle of the road. The man was waving his arms at a middle-aged woman cowering behind the wheel of a small car, pointing at what appeared to be his roadside fruit stall and shouting loudly. Darren could see a load of water melons strewn all over the road. He couldn't care less that the man with the checked cap was puffing out his cheeks and ticking off the old lady; all he wanted was for the bus to move off and get him to school.

The woman got out of the car and, from the passenger's side, out stepped a boy with a mess of dreads on the top of his head.

"Junior," Darren hissed under his breath. "What's he doing here?"

Darren watched as the boy walked towards the fruit seller. Darren recognised the walk as the rude bwoy skank. He'd seen

s at school walk like that. He
ney were cool — but he didn't
t Junior.

...om the top deck of the bus, Darren could see that Junior was a few inches taller than Mr Checked Cap. Whatever he was saying seemed to work, because the man doffed his cap at the woman, bowed slightly and started picking up the fruit. By this time, Junior had wrapped a comforting arm around the woman and led her back to her car.

"But sir," Darren pleaded as he danced around the teacher.
Mr Singh held his hand up, indicating for Darren to be quiet and keep still while he wrote down his name in his note pad.

It was a hopeless situation. After the bus had finally come to his stop, Darren had legged it to school. Seeing that the front gates were closed, he had quickly made for the side gates. He knew of a hole in the fence there, and if he acted swiftly he might have sneaked in without getting detention. He had known he was out of luck when the distinct red headgear of Mr Singh had appeared out of nowhere. Darren's heart had sunk.

"You know where to go after school," Mr Singh said unsympathetically as he ticked off the names of all the latecomers who were gathered around him. Everyone knew where to go for detention class; they were all familiar with the torturous route they would have to take to the new building at the other end of the school.

"But sir," Darren repeated, "it really wasn't my fault. It was that Junior."

"If I had a penny for every time someone said it wasn't their fault, I'd be a millionaire," the teacher replied coldly. Mr Singh was not prepared for any more excuses. He had heard them all over the years. He couldn't remember how many times latecomers would get down on their bended knees with their hands clasped as though in prayer, begging to be let off, every one of them giving him lame excuses about alarms not going off. One time a pupil had even had the gall to arrive in the afternoon, saying that he thought it was Saturday and hadn't realised until his mother came in from work. Can you imagine? It was such a far-fetched story that Mr Singh had given the boy the benefit of the doubt and let him off detention.

Looking at this lanky boy in front of him now, his lips curled up at the sides. He said to himself, "No." Darren James was a regular in his after-school class, there was no way he was going to let him off.

"You must like my classes, judging by how often you attend, James," Mr Singh said as his smile broadened and he rubbed his bearded chin. "Same time, same place." And with that he summoned another late student who was trying to sneak around the corner while he had been speaking to Darren.

Darren could have died. How could Mr Singh be so heartless? Didn't he realise that he was needed at the basketball practice that afternoon?

Darren was stone-faced as he pushed

open the main door to the school and, head bowed, shuffled along the corridor to his form room, dragging his school bag behind him.

Outside the form room was a row of grey lockers. Darren walked beside them, running a finger along the sides. He was close to tears. Stopping in front of one of the lockers, he turned the combination lock expertly. At that moment Mr Adams, the games master, walked around the corner whistling softly to himself. He stopped beside Darren as he recognised him.

"Oh, there you are, James," he said good-humouredly. He was wearing a red and black striped football jersey, a pair of white socks and trainers. "Don't forget practice, straight after school."

Darren gulped a mouthful of air into his lungs. He tried to speak but only managed to stammer. "But, sir..."

Mr Adams looked at him in a strange sort of way.

"What happens if we can't make it this afternoon?" Darren continued.

Mr Adams shook his head slowly. "No show, won't go." With that he walked away.

Darren groaned to himself as he trudged disappointedly to his form room.

Things just weren't going his way.

CHAPTER FOUR

"It was like the after-shock of a nuclear explosion," Miss Bird remarked in the staff room at break time. "In all my years of teaching it was the most disgraceful behaviour I have ever seen."

The other teachers who were seated in chairs around the room nodded their heads sympathetically. They could imagine what their colleague had seen.

"Which class was it today?" asked The Toupee as he tugged at the arms of his ill-fitting jacket.

"8W."

The Toupee nodded his head, taking care not to disturb the hairpiece that he wore. "I should have guessed. They are the worst of the bunch."

"Aren't you being rather hard on them?" Mr Robertson quipped, looking up from his newspaper. "You never see the good in them."

"Good in them!" The Toupee spluttered. "The only good thing about them is when they leave at half past three. Home time."

"I totally agree," Mr Singh chipped in, half-joking. "If it was left to me, I'd have them all in detention the whole day."

"Well, I suppose you're right," Miss Bird said to no one in particular. She slipped off her flat red shoes and rubbed the backs of her heels with her hand. Drummond Hill wasn't renowned for having the best-behaved kids in town — and the worst of the bunch was definitely 8W. Phyllis Bird's normally well-composed self had been severely tested as soon as she had entered their class room.

She had been passing on the way to her own first lesson, when she had been stopped by what sounded like the noise of rioting.

Their teacher had not yet arrived, and the class had been taking advantage of this unexpected freedom. Miss Bird had opened the door to find pupils sitting on tables throwing rolled up papers at each other; some were playing a game of 'had' around the room; a couple of others had even decided on giving an impromptu singing demonstration to a few of their classmates. One of the students had kicked another's bag, who in turn had shrieked, "My flour, you saddo! I need it for food technology class!" As the youngster had tried to rescue the errant rucksack, it was scooped up from the floor and swung round at shoulder height. The contents of the split flour bag had flown out of the rucksack and all over the teacher.

"Anyway, I think that we had better send the caretaker in to clean up the class room," Miss Bird now suggested.

Mr Robertson folded his newspaper on the coffee table in front of him. He had a confused look on his face. "Oh, I don't think that we should bother him over a few bits of paper littered on the floor and a dusting of flour. I'm sure that I can get the perpetrators to tidy up."

Miss Bird shook her head. "If only it were that simple. What really annoyed me was that they were so busy that none of them seemed to have noticed me at first. No one paid any attention to what I was saying. It was as if I was not there — invisible, almost."

"Hrumph!" The Toupee exclaimed. "Nothing is ever simple with that lot."

"No, especially when you get assaulted with bags of flour that totally ruin your favourite frock," the petite teacher complained. "Luckily Mr Adams had a spare track suit in the gym. It was very generous of him, but look... the colour doesn't even suit me!"

Mr Robertson shrugged this last comment away. He thought Miss Bird, a very attractive Asian woman, looked extremely athletic in the blue track suit with the stripes down the legs and arms. He would have said this much, but Miss Bird went on to explain how she had had to sit through her whole first lesson of the day wearing a spoiled dress.

Miss Bird's day continued in the same vein. When she arrived for her next lesson with 8B, she found it in mayhem. She was very disappointed. Furious, she went over to her desk and took out the biggest, heaviest dictionary she could find. Lifting it over her head, she let it drop to the floor.

Crash!!

The chattering stopped, as she had known it would. The pupils stared as though frozen in time. Everyone looked for the source of the noise. which, because of its suddenness, had abruptly cut off the din they had been making. One by one their faces changed as they recognised the face of the teacher who, curiously, was today wearing a blue track suit.

Miss Bird stood there, hands on hips, her broad, tanned face screwed up in a frown. Her red lips quivered as she searched for the right words to vent her anger. But no sound came out.

The kids knew that something was up; it

was not like Miss Bird to be upset. She was one of those teachers that all the children in the school wanted as their form teacher. She always had a smile and a friendly word for the pupils when she took them for any lessons. Her red dresses would brighten up any dreary afternoon. That was what she was noted for all over the school — wearing red. Her dresses were red, her shoes were red, even her lipstick and make-up were red. All the kids knew that if they wanted to get in her good books, all they had to do was buy her a packet of sweets with loads of red ones inside. But no amount of red sweets would please her now, judging by the look on her face.

"Right, now that I've got your attention," she said, regaining her composure. For a few moments there was a deathly hush from the whole class before she spoke again. "There is absolutely no need for this kind of behaviour, 8B. Think yourselves lucky that I don't put the whole class on report."

The class remained silent, and Miss Bird was about to launch into the real business of teaching when Darren walked in, head bowed. Miss Bird watched him as he dragged his feet on his way past her. She noticed that he did not have the usual lilt in his walk. "Nice of you to join us," she said, raising her eyebrows.

Darren didn't look up; he slid into his seat at the back of the class and placed his head in his hands, Mr Adams's words still ringing in his ears.

"Now, where was I?" Miss Bird said, placing her glasses back on her nose. "I've been asked by your regular teacher, who is off sick for the next few weeks, to arrange a project on the topic you have been studying."

"The Native Americans," called someone from the back of the class.

"That's right," Patrick Annette added. "Did you know that some tribes considered it more brave to touch a live enemy and get away, than to kill the enemy?"

"Excellent, Patrick," Mrs Bird complimented.

Patrick had a smug look on his face; it

wasn't every day that he got things right.

"Okay, I'm going to pair you off for this project," Miss Bird continued picking up a bundle of notes from her table and pulling out a sheet from it. She started arranging the pupils so that each boy was partnered with a girl. Eventually only Remi remained without a partner.

"Oh, well," the teacher said, "you'll have to carry out the project on your own." Remi shrugged; she preferred to work on her own anyway. She figured if anything went wrong she would have no one else to blame but herself.

"Settle down now," the teacher warned, "this is an important project for you. The mark that you receive from it will go a long way towards a high mark in your end of term assessment."

Meanwhile, in the headmaster's room, Mr Fredericks was in a meeting with a new boy and his guardian.

"This is the second school in less than a

year," the woman said as she opened her handbag. She fumbled around inside and took out a folded piece of paper. "Here is a number where you can reach me should anything happen," she said mysteriously, then she stood with some difficulty and offered Mr Fredericks a gloved hand.

The headmaster grabbed it in both hands and held it for a while before he shook it firmly.

"Junior," the woman said, turning to the still seated boy with the funky dreads, "I don't want you giving this nice gentleman any problems, do you hear?"

Junior nodded, remaining in the chair and staring intently at the carpeted floor. He was fed up with forever changing schools.

Mr Fredericks closed the door behind him after he'd said farewell to the woman. "Your aunt is a remarkable woman," he said.

The boy nodded again without lifting his eyes from the floor.

"Okay," Mr Fredericks continued with a hint of resignation in his voice, "I think I should introduce you to your new classmates."

"Good morning Mr Fredericks," chorused the pupils as the headmaster knocked and entered class 8B. The children had all stood up as they had been taught, and were looking at him expectantly. He nodded and waved a hand, indicating that they should sit. He whispered something to Miss Bird and turned to walk out of the door.

Miss Bird smiled softly at the boy that the headmaster had left standing near the blackboard. "Everyone, be quiet for a moment. This is Junior Brown and he's joining 8B today. I'm sure we all welcome him." She took a quick glance around the class. "Remi," she said as her eyes fell on the child's familiar features, "would you look after the new addition to the class?"

Remi nodded. "Yes, miss."

At the beginning of the lunch break, Darren stood with Anton and Tyrone by the bike sheds as they usually did. Darren had the headphones of his Walkman wrapped around his high-top, nodding his head to the beat and singing loudly.

"Well, what do you think about that Junior turning up here?" Tyrone asked.

Darren, unable to hear, continued to rock on. Tyrone had to shake him by the shoulders roughly before he removed his headphones reluctantly.

"What do you think of Junior turning up like that?"

Darren shrugged his shoulders in an unconcerned way. "Doesn't bother me."

Tyrone got the message loud and clear that no one was to know about the Street Fighter game.

"What doesn't bother you?" Remi asked, coming over. Her dark hair was pushed back at the front with a hair clip, exposing her coffee-coloured skin. Tenisha was standing behind her taller friend, beaming owlishly through her spectacles. It was a habit that got up her friends' noses. They could never figure out why she insisted on wearing them, even though they were practically falling to bits. Of course, if they had thought about it, they might have remembered that, what with her dad being on sick leave and half pay, Tenisha simply had to put up with what she had.

She was trying to hide the egg stain on the front of her sweater and was fiddling with the piece of plaster that held her glasses together. Her hair, in contrast to Remi's, was frizzy and was only kept in control by being plaited into cane rows.

"The new boy," Anton said.

Remi shrugged her shoulders. "He seems okay — quite cute as well."

Tenisha tried to hide a laugh behind her cupped hand. "You sound as though you're going off Darren."

Darren spun round. Remi was standing right behind him, her arms crossed around her chest. He couldn't find any words to say. His eyes met Tyrone's as he searched them for help.

"Did you notice the way she said that?" Darren whispered to Tyrone.

Tyrone shrugged his shoulders. "I didn't notice anything." He turned away and started waving at some boys playing basketball at the other end of the playground.

"I don't like that Junior, man. He's bad for me. If it wasn't for him I wouldn't have had detention," said Darren after a while.

"Why's that?"

"He was holding up the bus, posing around as though he was someone."

Tyrone turned to face him. "That's why you were late?" His voice held a twinge of disbelief in it.

"I don't know why he thinks he's so brilliant. How's it he's only been at the school for five minutes and everyone is going on about him as though he owned the place? All he is is a poser!"

Remi, who had been listening to what had been going on, said, "Why's it that you guys find it offensive that other people want to look good, huh? I suppose you'd prefer it if everyone wandered around looking terribly modest and sad."

"Yes, that's right," Tenisha quipped. "We are going to obliterate the word 'poser' from our vocab."

"Yes, the word to use is 'self expression'," Remi agreed.

Darren didn't answer, and after a moment Remi tugged at Tenisha's arm.

"We're outta here," she said as they walked off.

"Don't let them bug you, Darren," Anton said. "Why don't you tell us a joke?"

"You sure you want to hear one?"

"Yeah, why not?"

"Did you know that a pig is the only animal apart from humans that can get sunburned?" Darren said.

Tyrone groaned inwardly. He waited for the punchline but none came. Instead, Darren leaned on the wall with his arms crossed over his chest. "I saw it on a TV programme last night."

Tyrone's face showed that he was confused, but he nodded his head to show that he understood. A sharp blast of wind whistled past and Anton hunched his shoulders and shivered. "I wish the bell would ring so we can go in. It's freezing," he complained.

Darren turned slightly. He breathed out a short blast of air, watching the steam forming in front of him. "I know what you mean," he said.

Anton was hopping from one foot to the other. His hands were dug deep into his pockets as he tried in vain to keep warm. "The new boy seems kinda cool though," he mused. "You know, I think he had aftershave on."

Darren's eyes widened. "Huh!" he said. He moistened his dry lips by flicking his tongue over them. His mind drifted to the day some time in the future when he could put on his garms and spray his face with some Hugo Boss and come to school smelling sweet. He shook the thoughts from his head. That would be impossible. There was no way his pops would agree to that. "If I did that, all I'd hear would be 'What, you turn man now?' "

At that moment, Junior swaggered over to

join them.

"Let me borrow your headset," he said. He fixed Darren with a knowing stare, but neither boy let on that they had met before.

"I don't think so," was Darren's simple reply. He shook his head again, took the headset off his head and shoved it into his pocket.

"Jeez!" Junior exclaimed, turning to Darren's friends. "Your bredrin's tighter than a camel's backside in a sandstorm."

Anton and Tyrone burst out laughing, but they turned their heads away when they saw Darren glaring at them. Tyrone thought that the new boy was even funnier than Darren. Darren thought Junior was a jerk that went on as if he knew it all. Anyway, it wasn't as if he had to lend him his Walkman, was it?

CHAPTER FIVE

Darren soon forgot about Junior and how he had tried to show him up in front of his friends. He had other things on his mind. He still hadn't worked out how to get out of Mr Singh's detention class. But somehow he would *have* to get out of it because he couldn't afford to miss the crucial basketball practice.

He was standing outside the dining room with Tyrone when he turned to his friend for advice. "You've got to help me skip Mr Singh's class," he said.

Tyrone raised his hands above his head as they made their way into the noisy hall. He recognised the odour of curry wafting in his direction — not one of his favourite dishes, but he was hungry today. "You're asking for the impossible," he replied as he pushed his tray towards the servers. "If you ask me, I think your goose is cooked."

"So you're dissin' me now. Don't you think I can do it?"

"Oh, no, it's not that," Tyrone answered swiftly. He made his way to the table where they always sat and placed his tray on it before sitting down and tucking into his meal. Darren was close behind. "You know how Mr Singh always stays with his detention classes."

"That's why I've got to get away... I know where he keeps his detention book."

"Where?"

"In his desk — and I'm going to get it."

"I'm not sure that's a good idea, Darren. Why don't you forget about practice?"

"What, and miss the match? No way, José."

"Well I'm sorry, but I don't fancy your chances. And don't expect me to help you with it either."

"Don't need you anyway," Darren said sulkily.

After lunch, Darren made his way towards the first-floor room where Mr Singh kept his books. He knew, as did the rest of the school, that their turbaned teacher had a memory like an elephant. He never forgot a face. However, Darren banked on the fact that Mr Singh would be confused if he couldn't back a name with a face, if the book just 'disappeared'. It seemed far fetched, but it might just work...

After school, Darren and the rest of the basketball hopefuls were running around the athletics track as Mr Singh folded his arms behind his head.

"Quiet, boy!" he barked as one of the kids made a noise with his chair. He rocked gently back and forth in his chair, counting the mop of heads, his face creased into a smile. He liked being a teacher; he liked children — though he knew they weren't too fond of his detention classes.

"You know the rules in here. If you want something, raise your hand and wait until you are allowed to speak. I know that you all look forward to these classes, but you must remember what they are for."

He took a cursory glance over the heads that were buried in books. Mr Singh had been a teacher at Drummond Hill for longer than he could remember. He liked to see himself as a positive role model for his pupils. He recognised all the pupils, even if he didn't know them all by name and he prided himself on his ability to tell which ones were going to drop out or end up in trouble with the police.

One of his brightest pupils had even landed himself in prison. Mr Singh had known that the boy would eventually get into trouble; there had been something about him. One only had to take a stroll along the High Street and see some of the ex-pupils standing on street corners cussing each other and generally behaving badly to know that they were not all going to end up at university.

On more than one occasion Mr Singh, with a heavy heart, had turned the pages of the local paper to read a story about someone he had taught only a few years earlier being arrested by the police for one thing or another. And he'd seen how bright, eager and alert children in Year 7 would succumb to the pressures around them. He would listen to how their so-called friends had pressured them to do something illegal. That was why he was the way he was. He knew that he was thought of as too strict, but that was his way of trying to instill some sort of discipline and self-worth in the kids. It never ceased to amaze him how it was always the same kids that turned up late for school, the same ones who were sent to the Head's study, and the same ones who persistently forgot their homework and inevitably would end up in his detention class. Yet those same kids never seemed to forget their games kit, and had excellent recall of the big match on TV the night before or what shade of lipstick their favourite pop star wore on *Top of the Pops*. If only they would put as much effort into their school work. And whenever the parents were asked to come up to the school, the kids who had acted like monsters earlier would sit down meekly without saying a word. The parents would look on as though the teacher had lost his marbles or something.

Mr Singh's brow wrinkled as he studied the pupils in his detention class. Something didn't quite add up. He had somehow misplaced his notebook containing the names of all the pupils he had booked in that day.

"Err..." he stammered, "has anyone seen my detention book?"

A row of blank faces stared back at him. It had been left in his desk, he was certain of that, but for some unexplained reason it hadn't been there when he had checked earlier. He tried hard to remember the names he had written in it, and counting the heads again he was certain there was one missing. He racked his brains.

"Please, sir," a voice called from the back.

Mr Singh looked up and saw a child from Year 7, waving his arms frantically in the air.

"Yes, what is it?"

"I've finished. May I go and watch the basketball practice?"

Basketball practice? thought the teacher. He concentrated hard and a hazy image began to form in his mind. He pictured the face of a grinning boy with a gangling gait and a high-top hairstyle. The picture was complete as he remembered his earlier conversation with Darren James. He couldn't be certain, of course, but if there was one thing Mr Singh prided himself on, it was his memory. He wasn't like the rest of the teachers in school, who, as they got older, had difficulty remembering specific events.

"No. You must see this as a punishment," he answered the boy. "You'll have to wait until the rest have also completed their work." He looked out of the window. There were a few stragglers making their way out of the school. Towards the fences there was a group of pupils dressed in shorts and vests, doing some exercises by the running track. Mr Singh squinted as he tried to make them out. He could see the burly shape of Mr Adams, the sports teacher, standing in the centre of the group and gesticulating with one hand while bouncing a ball with the other. Everything seemed to fall into place when he saw Darren James jogging across the running track.

"Okay, sort yourselves out," Mr Adams said as he stopped bouncing the ball. The group of boys moved about haphazardly.

"Keep yourselves loose and warm." He jogged up and down on the spot, encouraging the boys to do the same.

"When are you going to name the team for the semi-finals?" Darren asked breathlessly.

"We're going to do some circuit training, after which I will name the team for the next game."

A loud whoop went up from those boys confident of being picked, and there were quieter cheers from the not-so-hopefuls.

"It's a foregone conclusion. I'll definitely get picked," Darren said, nudging Anton.

"Bet I won't," said Anton dejectedly.

Darren laughed as he did some stretching exercises, but the look on his face changed when he saw the familiar figure of the strictest teacher in the school walking towards them.

"Excuse me, Mr Adams, but I think you have an extra boy here."

The teacher turned to see the turbaned head of Mr Singh. Darren gulped as he realised the game was up.

"I believe you should be in my class," Mr Singh said, eyeing Darren up and down.

Darren knew that it was hopeless to argue. "Er, yes sir," he said.

"Follow me to Mr Fredericks's office, where we'll get to the bottom of this affair."

Darren, head bowed, dared not look at the faces of his sniggering team mates. He could feel Junior laughing and Tyrone's piercing stare that said 'I told you so'. He didn't want them to see the tears that were rolling down his cheeks. He turned his head slightly and caught the annoyed look on Mr Adams's face.

"I guess this means that I'm not in the team." He didn't even wait to hear the answer. He knew what it would be.

Although Tyrone was a little concerned about the welfare of his best friend, he would not have liked to swap places with him for a million pounds.

"I wonder what all that was about," said Anton.

Tyrone shrugged his shoulders. "He brought it all on himself — I warned him."

"But it's a shame that our best player won't be chosen."

"Yes, but perhaps it's not all doom and gloom if I get in," Tyrone said determinedly.

When they had completed their warm-ups, Mr Adams called the boys together.

"Only the fittest boys are joining the squad," he warned.

"I'm super fit!" cried someone from the back.

"All the same, I want you to run around the track a few times. Anyone who gets lapped will have to do an extra one."

This seemed fair to Tyrone. That was until he came around to lap Anton a second time.

Anton turned to look at him with a pleading look on his face. "No, no, not again," the chubby boy cried desperately. He already had an extra three laps to run and the thought of one more sent shivers down his spine.

"Come on, Miller! Run past him!" Mr Adams screamed from the edge of the track.

Tyrone saw that Anton was close to collapsing. He looked away guiltily as he gained speed and sprinted clear of his overweight friend. "I'm taking no prisoners, I will get into the team," he said under his breath.

Anton still had over four laps left to go as the other boys streamed into the gymnasium. While they sorted themselves out into teams, he ambled slowly around the circuit. He knew that he didn't have much chance of being picked for the team. What made him mad, though, was the way that his games teacher would always pick on him. He breathed a sigh of relief as he crossed the line to start his final lap.

Inside the hall Junior was playing a blinding game. No matter which position he was asked to play in, he seemed to have an uncanny knack of finding one of his teammates or scoring a basket from a seemingly impossible position. There was a lot of cheering, and some onlookers even went as far as saying that he was a better player than Darren. It didn't surprise Junior when, in the showers after practice, people came up to him saying, "You're sure of getting into the team, man." He shrugged. It was no big deal. He'd played better loads of times. He became very sarcastic. "Really? Do you think so? It's not exactly a hard team to get into."

"You're joking," Tyrone exclaimed, rubbing himself dry with his towel. "There are guys in this school that would sell their grandmother to play for this team."

"Is that so?" said Junior. "I suppose I'll

have to win the matches on my own, then."

"Whaddya mean?"

"Well, whenever anyone's got the ball they just pass to me and I'll do the rest. See ya," he said cheerily, and he made his way out.

CHAPTER SIX

Back in the privacy of his bedroom, Junior Brown sat uncomfortably on the edge of his bed, choking back the tears that were welling up behind his eyes. He hated himself for the way he felt. Although he didn't show it, he was proud of the reputation that he had. He realised that he was already known as a snappy boy rebel in this new school. He had read somewhere that people like him were misunderstood geniuses.

That's what he was — a genius. He was frustrated at the way he sometimes felt. Like that afternoon at basketball practice, dangerous, crazy. He enjoyed doing crazy things like taking the money that his aunt had given him that morning for lunch, skipping lunch and eating the sugar sandwiches he'd made instead. As far as he was concerned he was more sussed than all the weeds at his new school. Didn't his last science teacher say that sugar gave you energy? What better way to get it than by sprinkling sugar between two slices of bread?

Placing his hands behind his head, Junior lay down. He thought of his skilful display on the basketball field that afternoon. The kids patting him on the back after he had won the match didn't make him feel any closer to them. That was what he expected of lesser mortals. Then there was that girl, what's her name, the one who went around with the twerp he'd crucified on the video machines, the boy who still sported a high-top hairstyle. How totally uncool: a high-top. That went out with the dinosaurs.

Junior sighed deeply. Thinking of school only made him more depressed. If only he didn't get sick so often. He remembered clearly the day the doctors had told his aunt what was wrong with him. The long, unhappy look she had given him as he lay in bed with the long needles sticking out of his arms had been imprinted on his mind ever since. He was sure now that she was sorry she'd ever offered to look after him when his own mother couldn't be with him. Junior's mother still lived in Jamaica, where she had a very good government job. It was impossible for her to get an equivalent position in England. Because of Junior's poor health (at that time they didn't know exactly what was wrong with him) she thought it best to send him to her Aunt Sybil in London, what with the advanced medical procedures and treatment. His aunt was really his great aunt, and Junior felt that on the day the doctors spoke to her, he'd let her down; perhaps she wouldn't be able to cope and would no longer want to look after him. He'd started to become detached from everything, and that was when he started cutting himself off from other kids. He'd decided that the only person he could trust was himself.

He'd hated school anyway. It had always made him feel claustrophobic. The teachers would stand there talking to him as though he was an invalid, and it had eventually got so bad that he felt an increasing reluctance to get up in the morning. School for him was like being in a zoo. The kids in there reminded him of the caged animals you would see in Regents Park. The teachers were the keepers. Mr Fredericks? Well, he was the lion tamer.

Junior buried his head in his pillow. One thing that he wasn't bigger than was his illness. He hated sickle cell anaemia even more than he disliked school. Why did he have to have so much pain? Why couldn't one of the other kids have it? He could never find an answer to that. Even now, sitting on his bed, he was near to tears. Sometimes things seemed so meaningless to him. He had found that if he shut his eyes he would feel the walls closing in. The only place that he could escape to was a safe, empty, tiny room in his mind which provided him with some short relief from his pit of unhappiness.

Junior's mind went back over all that had happened with Darren at school, and how he had made him feel real small in front of his friends. Junior would have laughed if it wasn't for the pain that he was experiencing all over his body. He gritted his teeth hard and punched himself on the side of the head. He found that this sometimes helped to ease the pain, but it didn't seem to be working today. He cried out in agony as he received another jolt, but wished he hadn't when he heard a knock on his bedroom door.

"Junior?" his aunt called. "There's a young girl downstairs asking for you." She entered without waiting to be invited inside. "Is everything okay?"

"Yes, I was singing along to the music," he lied, flashing a toothy grin.

"But you don't look well. Are you sure that I shouldn't call an ambulance?"

Another searing pain shot through him. "No, don't do that. I'm fine. What does the girl want?"

"I don't know, Junior, maybe she's just

being friendly."

"Oh, all right. I'll be down in a minute."

His aunt gave him a long, hard stare before she closed the door and went downstairs to attend to the guest in the living room.

"If looks could kill," Junior mumbled to himself when the throbbing pain eased a little, "Darren would have had me buried."

It wasn't as though he had *wanted* the Walkman. It had simply been obvious to Junior from the moment he walked into class that Darren was the one he had to target. Darren was the class big man. If Junior was to take his place, he had to make Darren look bad. And yet, when he thought about it, perhaps Darren didn't deserve the rough treatment he intended for him. Despite the hi-top, the boy seemed a reasonable enough character. Junior could check for that.

He entered the living room. Remi was seated in the large settee looking through the photograph album.

She looked up excitedly. "I didn't know you entered for trampolining competitions," she said, pointing at a picture of Junior holding a trophy.

"Oh, that. It was nothing."

"Junior, you're so modest. And who is this hunk standing next to you?"

"I can't remember," he answered absently. "I only joined the team so I could get away from the freaks at the school," he added, mumbling under his breath. "Especially the one in the picture."

He remembered how the boy had strode up to him one day in the playground. Junior's knees had started trembling as he feared the worst. His heart had raced as he wondered whether or not the older lad was going to rearrange his face for him.

"I'm dead," he'd thought. He'd cringed and closed his eyes, tensing his body expectantly. But then he'd felt an arm around his shoulder. Opening first one eye and then the other, he'd stared up at the face in front of him.

"How do you get to do those moves?" the

boy had asked.

"I can't..." he'd stammered.

"Go on, tell me," the taller boy had begged, rubbing Junior's hair.

"I can't. My dad told me not to," Junior had lied. He didn't feel like telling anyone how he had worked out for all those hours. Anyway, it wasn't as if you could just tell someone and that was it.

The older boy had pleadingly looked at him once more before he shrugged his shoulders and walked away, taking a last look at his younger school companion.

The pain returned — sharply. It sped through his body like a bullet. He punched himself again on the side of the head as it brought him close to tears.

Remi looked on in a concerned manner. "What's up?"

"Nothing. I feel like yesterday's chewing gum, that's all." Standing slowly, he pulled himself up and walked gingerly over to the CD player at the side of the room. Searching through the large collection of disks, he found one and slipped it into the machine.

The music pumped. He sat on the edge of the settee, switching on the TV with the remote control pad he had in his hand. The set flickered into life and the music synchronised with the pictures on the screen. The tune was by TLC, 'Waterfalls', and the video had come with the CD. Left Eye singing away reminded him of one of the girls from his last school who had come up to him in the playground, soon after the incident with the older boy.

"Do you know, she reminds me of my last girlfriend," he said above the music.

"Who does?"

"Left Eye. That was why I had to leave my old school."

"You had to leave because she looked like a girl in a band?"

"No, she followed me everywhere I went. Wherever I turned, there she was, making eyes at me."

"I bet you have that problem all the time," Remi said mischievously.

Jeez, Junior thought to himself, she seems to be going on like the rest of those silly girls.

"It was so bad," he said, "that I'd deliberately avoid going in the same direction as her."

"Some girls are like that," Remi answered.

Junior continued. "It got so that she went around and told all her friends we were going out. Before I knew it, all the girls were crowding round me and following me everywhere."

"I once had a similar experience," Remi confided.

"Oh yeah?" Junior wasn't really interested in what she had gone through, but he found that talking kept his mind off the pain. So he tried to keep his mind on the story that Remi was telling him.

However, his mind was drifting to the past. It had been difficult to resist the compliments he got. It wasn't every day that you had a posse of girls checking for you, especially when they don't do it out of sympathy. Even the headmaster had admired him. The first time that the Head offered him a lift home he'd refused, but then he'd thought, What the heck! So what if the Head only treats me nice because he wants the school in the area gymnastics championships?" The school had been getting a lot of publicity in the newspapers.

Junior's aunt had been so happy when the Head dropped him off, and she went on for days afterwards about how glad she was that Junior was settling down at the school. Even his mother sent him a special card. Everything would have been fine if the other kids had felt the same way about the Head driving you home in his car after school. There were loads of names for anyone thought of as a teacher's pet, but there had been some new ones invented for Junior. The headmaster's pet!

The TV screen went blank as the video ended. The pain came back with greater force than before. When it eased a little, Junior thought about how things had started to go wrong. He decided to change the disc.

"So why did you stop competing?" Remi asked, following the boy's movements across the room with her eyes.

"I don't know. I just did, that's all."

He should have told her about the tournament, the final tournament.

He was competing in an important competition, all his friends had been in the crowd cheering, his girlfriend Michelle Beaumont at the front, waving.

"Go get 'em!" she had called. Michelle, the prettiest girl in the school, and Junior, the most popular boy: what a combination. It was his big moment. He had arrived at the auditorium amid loud cheers. When he had stepped in front of the judges, he knew almost straight away that he was going to win. The rest of the competitors' routine hadn't matched up to his. Even so, when he heard his name being called, it had felt as though he was in the middle of a dream.

"With a score that has never been gained before," the announcer had said over the public address system, "the overall champion, the new junior trampolining champion of the South East — Junior Brown!"

His games teacher had prodded him in the small of the back. "That's you, Junior," he'd said, as he hugged him tightly and lifted him up in the air. He'd pushed him on to the platform.

"Big up to the max," screamed some school friends of his who were waving banners from the back of the hall.

"Give them an extra pose, and smile," his games teacher encouraged.

Junior had looked around. He was alone up there on the platform. The brightly coloured sash had been placed around him. Up in the stands, Michelle and the rest of the fans were singing along to the tune they were playing: 'Simply The Best'. Junior had smiled broadly, his pearly white teeth gleaming in the bright lights. He was getting dizzy with all those lights, the cheering and the flash of the cameras. He had never felt so happy in his life.

Then it had happened. He had known what was going on before he collapsed. It was always the same. His breath was coming in short gasps. He felt like puking, his head was spinning. Then, before he could cry out, he was looking up, the bright lights blurring in his vision. There were cries of fear from the crowd and he thought he saw Michelle turning her face away in embarrassment, though he must have imagined it because all he could really see were the blurred lights in the ceiling. Blinding. Then, from far away, he could make out what the muffled voices were saying. "I wonder if he's on drugs..."

A voice inside him had wanted to scream out, "No! It's not drugs!"

Why did it always happen to him?

After all that, he had insisted on leaving the school immediately.

Junior shook his head as he remembered he had company. "Anyway," he said, facing Remi, "why did you come over?"

"I just came to say hello because, if we're sitting next to each other, we'll probably be doing some projects together. I thought it would help if we knew each other a bit. Is that okay?"

Junior nodded. "Yeah, it's okay," he said.

But Remi wasn't sure that he meant it.

CHAPTER SEVEN

The next day at school Darren was convinced that he was being tortured by everyone at school.

Even Philip Hector had managed to get into the basketball team. "Move yourself," Darren had said when smelly Philip had wafted over to tell him the good news. He wished silently to himself that he could die. To make matters worse he had a maths lesson later which he always found really boring. The only way he could get through maths was by getting Tyrone to help him. He could always count on his best friend to slide his exercise book across the desk in such a way that Darren could copy it without Miss

Bird noticing.

He couldn't wait for the day when he did not have to come to school any more. Instead of boring maths he would be able to stay at home and play with his Nintendo every day. School had got so bad that he had started to hate it. If only he could turn the clock back twenty-four hours... If he could start over again he would just go to Mr Singh's detention class and miss games practice. But it was too late now.

After a severe lecture from Mr Fredericks the day before, he had confessed to taking the detention book. The Head was particularly hot on stealing. It was bad enough that he'd telephoned Darren's dad about how he'd misbehaven.

When the last hymn at morning assembly had been sung, Mr Fredericks stood at the front, staring. The whole of the lower school shifted uneasily as they waited to be dismissed.

"Darren James!" Mr Fredericks bellowed, searching the faces of the seated kids. "Darren James, stand up boy!"

Darren screamed inwardly as the whole of his class turned to stare at him, exposing him so that he had nowhere to hide. He stood uneasily, his head bowed and his hands clasped behind his back.

"I want all of you to turn and look at that boy," Mr Fredericks said, pointing his finger at the culprit.

Darren shifted his feet. He knew what was coming, but he hadn't thought the Head would go this far.

"There is a boy that thought he could set his own rules in the school. There is a boy that thought he could hoodwink his teachers!"

A gasp went up from the assembled pupils.

"I want you to take a good look at him," the Head continued, "because you won't be seeing much of him after school from now on."

Darren held his breath expectantly, wondering what extra punishment he was going to have dished out to him.

"And when you do happen to catch a

glimpse, you will see him going around the school collecting any rubbish that is lying around."

What's this?! Darren screamed to himself. Who does he think I am, a rubbish collector? His legs were telling him to up and walk out of the assembly hall, to get away from the two hundred pairs of eyes that were staring at him. Don't be so silly, warned a voice in his head. He lowered his eyes and listened to Mr Fredericks going on about how he had taken Mr Singh's detention book in order to try to skip detention.

"This boy lied and stole," bellowed the Head. "I won't tolerate such behaviour in my school."

Give it a rest motor mouth! Darren thought. What are you on about, *your* school? I wonder how much you paid for it? He didn't hear much after that. All he was wondering was when he could sit down again and why Mr Fredericks was going on so much because of some small prank.

Just when he thought that his legs would give way, the Head dismissed the lower school. Darren groaned as he rubbed the backs of his legs and filed out behind Tyrone.

Dinner time did not improve things.

"Look at that," Tyrone exclaimed suddenly as they sat down with their trays of food.

Darren followed his friend's finger and saw Remi and Tenisha walking, trays in hand, to where Junior was sitting. Junior's face had a broad grin on it.

Darren grunted. "It looks as if that bwoy has never heard of a mirror," he said, nodding his head in Junior's direction.

"Why do you say that?"

"Well, look at him. His hair is not in place, his shirt seems as if he adjusted it at a right angle, and if that spot gets any bigger..."

"Mmm..."

"Have you heard the joke about the chicken and the road?" Darren asked, trying to sound excited.

Tyrone seemed not to have heard him, because he continued to look over at Junior's table where now a crowd had gathered. He wondered what could be going on, but didn't get much time to think about it before Patrick Annette came over and placed his tray in front of him.

The boys gritted their teeth and scowled at the lanky lad who had the nerve to come and sit at their table. Patrick was one of those kids who thought they were cool, when in fact they were real butters. A sap. He was the kid that the expression 'butters' had been invented for — at least that was what Darren thought. He didn't dress particularly well: the clothes that he wore were butters, especially his school uniform. Darren wondered to himself how the beanpole kid could look so weedy. He could understand that maybe Patrick couldn't afford to buy any nice garms, but he could not figure out for the life of him how anyone could look so utterly geek-like in a black jacket, white shirt and striped tie.

Patrick's creased shirt dangled tail-like from under his jacket. The shoes on his sockless feet looked as though they had kicked many stones on countless pavements. Even his hairstyle is butters, Darren thought. He sported one of those cuts that was half-way between an Afro and a wet-look. Patrick reminded Darren of Michael Jackson on an off day. He couldn't help but laugh out loud as he thought about this.

Patrick Annette screwed up his face and looked at Darren quizzically. He couldn't see what was so funny.

"Guess what?" Patrick said in a matter-of-fact way. His eyes shifted from Darren to Tyrone, searching, hoping that one of them would take the bait. Finally he could wait no longer. "Junior Brown has been made captain of the basketball team."

Darren's heart skipped a beat. It was bad enough that he was not going to be in the team, but making Junior the *captain?* Things couldn't get any worse. He jabbed his fork into his meal and took a mouthful, chewing slowly as the shock of what he had been told sunk home. Junior had been given *his* responsibility. It wasn't fair. It wasn't as if Junior had been at the school for long.

"Junior bloomin' Brown, I hate you," he hissed under his breath.

Darren was still feeling fed up with life when he was standing with the rest of the crew in the playground behind the bike sheds.

"Look at him," he said, pointing at Junior Brown. "Don't you just hate the way he looks?"

"I will say one thing," Tyrone said, looking over at the group of girls that were gathered around their new classmate, "you have to big him up. Some of the things he says are well cool." He blew on his cold fingers and jabbed them deep into his pockets.

Darren gave Tyrone a sideways glance. "Ty! You were there when we were playing on the video machines; when he just pocketed my money, like it was his. How could you want to big him up?"

"Look, Darren, you've gotta accept that he was beating you on the machine. That money *was* his."

"It sounds as though he's fooled you too."

"No, it's just that he comes out with some brilliant lyrics."

"I've heard them all before. All he is is a show off." He looked back towards his rival. Remi walked nonchalantly over to where Junior was holding court. Darren could not be sure, but he imagined that she was fluttering her eyelashes a little too much at the smiling new boy. He punched a fist into his open palm in frustration. "Anyway, I don't trust him."

"Why's that?"

"Well, mainly because of what he did at the leisure centre, of course. But apart from that, we don't know very much about him. I mean, where does he come from, where does he get his garms from, eh?"

Tyrone chuckled. "I don't know, but are you sure you're not getting jealous?"

"Why would I be jealous of someone as boring as him?"

The two boys cleared their plates and returned the empty trays to be stacked. "He has been made captain of the team," Tyrone continued.

They made their way to the playground, and seeing Anton they went over to join him. Darren was really annoyed at his mate's last comment.

"Someone comes waltzing in bigging himself up and you lot are all over him. Look at Remi for instance. Well, I'm different. I'm not fooled by him. I intend to get to the bottom of it."

Tyrone shrugged. "He seems safe to me."

Darren lowered his voice when he saw Remi, Tenisha and Junior walking over to them. "Junior Brown is soon going to be history," he said to himself.

A broad grin spread over his face. Gritting his teeth, he feigned surprise. "Hi!" he said cheerfully. He offered his fist to Junior in greeting. They touched. Darren thought for a second that Junior's grin was spread even wider than his own.

Then Junior put a friendly arm around Darren's shoulder. Tyrone looked on uneasily, shifting his feet. He felt a twinge of jealousy when he saw this. It wasn't like Darren to let anyone but his best friend put an arm around him.

"Hey," Junior said in a taunting voice. He patted Darren on the shoulder in a consoling manner. "I really feel bad about what happened earlier."

Darren looked dubious but he shook his head forcefully. "I don't know what you mean."

Junior looked around at the group of friends. "You must be totally cheesed off now you're out of the team."

"I'm not really that bothered. I needed a rest anyway."

Junior ignored him. "Then there's you and Remi being an item and all. I thought that you would be a little sore."

Remi flushed. "But me and Darren were never an item," she said defensively.

Darren shifted his feet uncomfortably. "That's right," he said in an unconvincing voice, "we're just good friends."

Junior stood feet apart, his hands dug deep into his pockets. His shoulders were hunched as they combated the cold wind that blew across the playground. He leaned towards Darren and whispered in his ear. "Don't you think that this school is full of geeks?"

"Unhh?!"

"Well, I've only been here two days and it's just like the rest of them I've been to — boring."

Hearing the new boy sounding off about the school didn't quite add up — and, anyway, who did he think he was, knocking Drummond Hill? Darren could see the moment as an opportunity to show Junior that he wasn't as clever as he made out to be. As far as Darren was concerned, Junior was second to him in the stakes of school life.

"There are some interesting things that you don't know about this school," replied Darren.

Junior rose to the challenge. "Like what?" He took his hands from his pockets and crossed them over his chest importantly.

"Did you know..." Darren began in a superior tone. He looked around to see

Tyrone listening keenly to the conversation. "Did you know that if you stand by the air vents outside the science lab, you can hear everything that goes on in the girls' changing rooms?" Darren declared his revelation with a flourish of his arms. He thought he saw a glint of admiration in Junior's eye.

Behind him he heard a little gasp. Turning his head, he saw Tenisha with her hands cupped over her mouth. Darren's gaze shifted to Tyrone, who was trying his best to avoid his friend's eyes by staring down to the concrete floor and blowing a blast of warm air into his hands before rubbing them together vigorously. Anton had his back to them. "I'm freezing," he said to no one in particular.

Remi's face contorted into an expression of anger. "So, whenever you ask to be excused from class to use the loo," she said in an incredulous manner, "what you're really saying is, 'Miss, I feel like eavesdropping on other people's conversations.' "

Junior broke into guffaws of laughter

along with Anton and Tyrone. All three were slapping each other on the back as they flicked their fingers in appreciation. "Wicked!" they cried simultaneously.

Darren couldn't see what was so funny, it was only an observation he had made the other day, and one he had imagined Junior would have been happy to hear.

"Now it's my turn," Junior said as he wiped a tear from his eye.

Darren nodded, silent contempt in his eyes.

"Repeat after me: Oh Wah..."

Darren's mind raced. Why would Junior want him to repeat such a silly word? It crossed his mind that he should call a halt to the whole shebang.

His decision was made for him when he heard Remi's voice. "Come on, Darren," she coaxed. "Say it." There was an impatience in her voice and she dug her elbow in his ribs to encourage him.

Darren shrugged his shoulders and stomped his feet; the cold had got into his bones and his ears felt like someone had sliced them with a razor blade. He wished the bell would sound for the end of break.

"What do you want me to say?"

"Oh Wah."

"Oh... Wah," Darren repeated slowly.

"Tajek Kiam."

"Tajek Kiam," Darren said, wondering what sort of stupidness Junior was plotting.

"Now say it together, and fast," Junior said as he gave a sideways wink to Remi.

"Oh what a jerk I a—" Darren's voice trailed off at the end of the sentence. He realised too late what he was saying. It seemed that all his friends had heard it as well, because they were now falling about laughing.

Darren could have thumped Junior. It wasn't every day someone was able to get the better of him. His mind raced as he tried to think of a good comeback, but he couldn't. He knew then that he would have to get even with Junior if it was the last thing he did.

Darren was thinking how best to do it when the bell sounded to signal the end of break. He moved off sharpish, but could hear Tyrone and Anton still having little bursts of the giggles.

Just then Philip Hector rushed over.

"Hey, Darren, you couldn't lend me three pounds till I see you at the club tonight, could you?" He offered a fist in greeting.

"What do you need it for?"

"It's the ghastly school dinners. I couldn't handle it today."

"Sorry man, no can do," Darren said, shaking his head a little more vigorously.

"Aw c'mon, D. I'm starving."

Darren waved a dismissive hand at the disappointed boy.

"But Darren, you always lend me money!"

This was true. But Darren was broke today and he didn't want to let on.

"Hold it!" Junior had overheard the conversation. "Perhaps I can be of some help."

"Unhh?!"

"Yeah, that's right," Junior said as he approached them. "What have you got there?" Junior indicated with a nod of his head at Philip's hand.

"Oh, this. It's only my Gameboy."

"No, no, no," Junior said, walking towards the sweaty boy. He took the hand-held computer toy from him. "Don't look at it as *only* a Gameboy," Junior continued. "Look at it as a way to have a slap-up meal at the chip shop later."

"How am I supposed to do that?" Philip was confused.

"Well, you let me have the Gameboy, and I give you the three pounds that you were asking for."

"No, I don't think so."

"What you sayin'? It's a bargain — after all, it is an old game."

Philip considered this. "Well... I'm not sure."

Junior saw his chance and seized it. "Look, if you don't want to do business, that's okay. I thought I was doing you a favour, that's all." He made to walk away.

"Okay, I'll do it," Philip said quickly.

Junior stopped in his tracks and turned, grinning broadly. Grabbing the proffered machine, he dug his hands deep into his pockets and dropped some coins on the floor.

Philip made a dash for them as they rolled about. "Hey!" he called loudly. "There's fifty pence short."

"What's that?" Junior smiled.

"You've only given me two pounds fifty. Where's the rest?"

"Oh, didn't I tell you? That was interest for not taking up my offer the first time."

Philip mumbled something under his breath as he walked away towards the far end of the playground.

"Don't forget to let your friends know," Junior shouted at the disappearing back. He turned to face the others. "Another satisfied customer," he said, showing off by pulling out a large wad of notes from the inside of his blazer.

"Wow, where did you get all that?" exclaimed Remi.

"Here and there," answered Junior Brown mysteriously. "If I can make money, invest money, scheme money, save money — I'm in there, man."

By now the playground was almost empty as pupils were returning to their lessons.

Darren's head was spinning. He hated Junior for the way he had cheated Philip. After all, Philip was one of his regular customers. Quickening his pace, he headed towards the double swing doors that led into the school. Remi was walking a few paces ahead of him with Junior. All Darren could think about at that moment was how he was going to get back at the new boy.

"Junior is dark," Anton whispered.

"Yes, if you think being an ugly saddo is cool," said Darren through gritted teeth. As far as he could tell, Junior was carrying on too smart for his own good. He would have to get his comeuppance. But how? Darren was still pondering this as he hurried to his next lesson.

CHAPTER EIGHT

That evening at dinner, Darren and Tyrone sat expectantly while Yvonne and Marcia, their mothers, talked. Lester was out playing squash with work friends. Surprisingly Patricia had offered to accompany him, most likely to con more money out of him, Darren thought suspiciously.

The two boys shifted in their seats, hoping to catch their mothers' eye. Darren had been boasting throughout the meal, challenging Tyrone's skills on the Street Fighter computer game.

"I'm so skilful I could lick you with my eyes closed," he taunted.

"You won't be saying that when Ryu gets

extinguished yet again," countered Tyrone.

Darren's face was contorted in anger. "Ryu is invincible in my hands; he never fails in his mission to repel all challenges."

Tyrone rolled his eyes. "Almost all, Darren," he said pointedly. "And tonight you will lose again!" He nudged his friend gently in the ribs. Darren got the message and wolfed down the remains on his plate.

Making their excuses, the two boys rushed out of the dining room to Darren's room upstairs.

When morning came the next day, Darren had totally forgotten about Junior. He was still on a high from the beating he'd given Tyrone on the computer the night before. He had an extra skip to his walk as he made his way into school. But that morning events were to take over in a way he could only in his sweetest dreams have planned.

It was Harvest Festival. "Will this class please bring their provisions for the elderly to the front?" ordered Mr Robertson, who was organising the collection.

There was a shifting of tables and chairs as the pupils made their way to the front of the class, placing tins of tomato soup, biscuits and other foodstuffs in the two boxes by the door.

Mr Robertson beamed. "I see that your parents have been very generous this year. These provisions will be very welcome among the elderly people in this area." The bell rang for assembly. "Okay, make your way out in an orderly fashion. Darren and you, Junior, take these boxes into the hall, please."

The two boys followed the teacher out of the classroom, carrying the large boxes of fruit, eggs, flour, canned soup and vegetables. They passed through the heavy swing doors that led into the assembly hall, where the lower school was gathered, singing 'All things bright and beautiful'. Mr Robertson was striding in front with Junior, Darren walking close behind. Suddenly Darren's eyes twinkled, as he realised how he could make the new boy look a real twerp. His grin widened as they made their way slowly down the aisle, arms straining under the weight of their provisions. Junior, unsuspecting, beaming with pride, walked steadily forward. Darren saw his chance. This was his opportunity to get even with Junior, and he seized it without thinking. He snaked out a foot. In his haste to stop from falling face-first onto the floor, Junior sent his basket of goods into the air, stretching out a hand to break his fall. Quick-thinking pupils in the choir, who stood in front, ducked in time to avoid being hit by flying tins and flour, but Mr Singh, obviously not as fast as his charges, stared open-mouthed as a box of eggs came flying in his direction. He seemed paralysed as he watched the eggs sailing though the air towards him. He didn't even have a chance to give the pupils one of his icy stares. The whole of the assembly burst into instantaneous laughter as — *splat!* — Mr Singh looked down on his newly purchased suit covered in sticky egg yolk.

"What the...!"

Mr Fredericks had looked up from his hymn book by now and was peering over the top of his spectacles. Darren looked at him sheepishly and imagined that he saw the slightest hint of a smirk develop on the Head's normally serious face. The turbaned teacher scowled angrily at Junior as he took a hanky from his pocket and attempted to clean his jacket.

Junior was not making matters any better, because he was by now clawing desperately at Mr Singh's foot in an attempt to pull himself up. But the floor was slippery and he kept falling back down.

Mr Singh was having none of it, and he frantically tried to shake the clinging boy off, vibrating his leg as though there were a rabid dog on the end of it.

Darren, acting innocently, reached out a comforting hand. Junior made to grab hold of it, but in his haste he trod on a tin of soup that had fallen out of his basket.

What happened next was the highlight of the whole morning for Darren. Junior fell again, this time managing to grab Mr Singh around the waist. The teacher had no alternative but to follow his pupil on to the varnished floor. As the teacher fell, legs askew, the seat of his trousers ripped, exposing to the whole of the lower school his natty boxer shorts.

A whoop of delight rose at once from the onlookers. Mr Singh, stone-faced, muttered incoherently as he walked out of the hall. Meanwhile, Miss Bird helped Junior up and put her arm around him with what seemed to most of the gathered assembly to be more care than he really deserved.

It took Mr Fredericks almost ten minutes to restore order.

"Can you believe it?" Anton exclaimed to Tenisha during first break. "Mickey Mouse underwear!"

As far as Darren was concerned, that was the end of the matter. Mr Singh had got his comeuppance for getting Darren thrown off the basketball team, and he was even with Junior, so that was that. Or so he thought.

Darren was standing by his locker after break when Junior strode angrily towards him.

"You're out of order," he spat venomously.

"What do you mean?" Darren said, a look of surprise on his face.

"Don't make out you are so innocent. I know you tripped me on purpose."

Darren turned to move, but Junior blocked his path.

"I think you're getting paranoid," Darren said as he pushed past.

Without a word of warning, Junior grabbed Darren by the shoulders and headbutted him on the bridge of the nose.

"Arrrghh!" cried Darren. "What was that for?"

Junior didn't answer. He made to punch Darren, and would have done so if Patrick Annette, who had been watching, had not grabbed his arm.

"Mr Fredericks is coming," he whispered.

Junior peered up nervously and saw the figure of the headmaster walking in their direction. He panicked and dropped his arm, patting Darren on the shoulder as he did so.

"You're lucky," he said, waving a threatening finger. "I'll see you behind the bike sheds after school." And with that he stormed off.

Darren's nose throbbed. He shuddered as he watched Junior disappearing to his next class. He hadn't planned to have a fight with him. He had imagined that his little prank would have simply blown over, but Junior obviously was not going to leave it at that.

"You okay?" Patrick asked.

"Yes," Darren muttered, shrugging the geeky boy's arm off his shoulder. He owed Patrick a favour for having saved him from a hiding, but that didn't mean he had to get up close and personal.

It seemed to Darren that the other pupils at the school were taking the situation and making it grow out of all proportion. The only topic of conversation on their lips for the rest of the day was the fight that was to take place after school. Patrick, the school gossip, had seen to that. Even the teachers sensed that something was afoot. They could tell by the way their pupils whispered behind cupped hands when they should have been studying, and by the notes they glimpsed being passed under tables. They had learnt from experience that when the kids carried on like this there was usually something cooking.

Darren did not want to keep the appointment with Junior, and was relieved to discover a way out when he passed Mr Robertson and The Toupee outside the staff room.

"I sense there's something going down with the pupils," The Toupee said as he opened the door to step inside.

"Yes, I've noticed it too. We shall have to keep an eye on them for the rest of the day."

Darren could not believe his ears. He had not been up for a fight, but had not had the courage to say so. Without being aware, the two teachers had now given him an escape route. He walked with a bright skip to search for his opponent.

"Oh, there you are," he said when Junior found him coming out of the gym. Junior was dressed in a pair of black lycra cycling shorts and a skimpy burgundy basketball vest. He had his arms crossed over his chest in a way that made them seem larger than they were. Darren noticed Junior's muscles and took a deep gulp before he spoke.

"Hey, what's up?" he said jovially, offering his fist in greeting.

Junior scowled at him and gave a look of disdain at the proffered fist. He declined the peace offering.

"I think that we should call off the fight."

"Why's that?" Junior said menacingly.

"All the teachers know about it."

"No problem — we'll just change the venue."

"That's what I was thinking," Darren said with a heavy heart.

"That's okay then. See you down the rec straight after school!" And with that Junior turned away and made for the showers.

"This isn't my day," Darren groaned inwardly as he skulked away.

As soon as the final bell went to signal the end of school, there was a mad dash for the doors from almost every class in the lower school. Teachers looked up concerned as they attempted to hand out homework. Lockers were opened, emptied and locked hastily as everybody made a frantic rush to get out of the school building. It seemed like any normal end of day at Drummond Hill School, except that instead of making their way towards the gates, all the pupils seemed to be heading in the opposite direction — towards the bike sheds where to their horror they were met, not by the sight of Darren and Junior punching the daylights out of each other, but by Mr Singh.

Meanwhile Darren and Tyrone entered the recreation ground. Darren took a nervous peek over Tyrone's shoulder as they made their way to the prearranged spot underneath the weeping willow trees.

"I think you need your head examined," Tyrone said.

"Why's that?" asked Darren.

"Well, Junior might be short, but he's really fit. And he's angry, man."

Darren would have said something to Tyrone about him not having enough faith in his fighting skills if it hadn't been for the shout that came from the row of privet hedges opposite. Both boys turned around to see Junior calling.

"What's he doing here?" Junior asked, pointing.

"Don't worry about him," Darren said dismissively, "he's just chillin'."

Junior eyed Tyrone suspiciously as he circled Darren. "Anyway, I'm not really that bothered. I can whop the two of you with one hand tied behind my back," he boasted.

"In your dreams."

"Yes, and what will you do to stop it?" Junior said, stepping closer, toe to toe, so that his nose was almost touching Darren's.

Darren shoved him away with his hands.

"If you come any closer, you'll soon see," he threatened, kissing his teeth.

"I'm shaking in my shoes." Junior held his hand in a limp manner.

"What you bigging yourself up for? If you carry on like that you won't be standing in your boots much longer, isn't that so, Ty?" Tyrone did not answer. "Here, hold my jacket." Darren took off his jacket and handed it to his friend. He undid his tie and loosened the top button of his shirt.

"Come on, you two. Don't you think you've taken it all a little too far?" Tyrone pleaded.

In the moment that Junior turned to reply to Tyrone, Darren saw his chance and brought his right fist down hard, hitting his foe on the cheekbone just below his left eye. Junior, who had not been expecting it, staggered backwards. Darren, meanwhile, had raised his other fist and swung it in a wide arc. It landed with a dull thud in Junior's stomach.

"Oof!" Junior cried as he bent himself over, gulping desperately for air.

From the corner of his eye he could see Darren coming towards him, ready to finish him off. He raised a leg defensively in the air and kicked out in the direction of his oncoming opponent. It caught Darren full in the mouth.

Darren licked his lips and tasted the saltiness of his own blood. He had seen Junior aiming the kick at him, but he had been charging in so fast that it was impossible for him to avoid it. He held his face in his hands as Junior rushed in and started to rain a flurry of blows on his head, in his stomach and on virtually every exposed part of his body.

He felt faint and could feel himself passing out as Tyrone jumped on Junior's back and held his arms to stop him from hurting Darren any more. But Tyrone couldn't control both boys at once, and the fact that Junior was being restrained gave Darren his chance. He scrambled to his feet, and with the last ounce of strength in his arms and legs he started systematically to punch and kick Junior.

Junior was taking a real good hiding now, but he was not making any sound. Instead he just stared back at Darren defiantly.

"That's enough, Darren," Tyrone said angrily, as he stepped away.

Junior was holding his chest, groaning. Even though Darren had laid into him good and hard, the wiry boy seemed to be in more pain than Darren had expected.

"I don't think he looks too good," said Tyrone. "Maybe there's something wrong with him."

"Don't worry about him, he got what he deserves. Come on, let's go." Darren took a last look at the whimpering boy before he disappeared through the privet hedges with Tyrone following close behind. Darren offered him his fist. Tyrone felt sick.

They walked briskly along the street, Darren taking care that his spoiled shirt was hidden under his jacket. They had one scary moment when they spotted The Toupee coming out of the Post Office on the High Street, but they ducked sharply in a shop doorway until he was out of sight. The remainder of the journey home, Darren was going on about how Junior was lucky that his face hadn't been rearranged.

"If it wasn't for the fact that you pulled me off, who knows what I would have done to him."

Tyrone did not answer.

"I'm going to be even more destructive on the computer games later, eh?"

Tyrone was glad as they approached Wood Lane. He was getting fed up with the way his best friend was going on; he also wanted to get on with the homework that they had been given earlier.

"See you about six then?" Darren said cheerily.

"Yeah," Tyrone replied coldly, a shiver running down his spine

In his bedroom, Darren knew he was safe from Junior Brown and his taunting, and the lopsided grin that he would flash at Darren when their paths crossed in the corridor or the playground at school. He didn't have to worry about the sideways look that Junior would give him as he accidentally-on-purpose bumped into him. Junior had done that to him on countless occasions. If he complained, Junior would just laugh and kiss his teeth at Darren and say that there wasn't enough room in Drummond Hill School for the both of them.

Yes, Darren concluded, Junior Brown deserved everything that he got today.

CHAPTER NINE

On Saturday the sun peeped briefly through the autumn clouds for the first time that week. As previously arranged, Darren, Tyrone, Remi and Tenisha had met on the canal bank. Darren and Tyrone sat near the water's edge, watching as their tiny floats bobbed gently in the water. They had their Los Angeles Raiders caps pulled low over their eyes.

Darren reached into his fishing bag and grabbed at a handful of maggots which he threw into the water. Remi and Tenisha were sitting a few feet away on a grass mound underneath a weeping willow tree. The girls were dressed differently, though they both had scarves wrapped around their necks. Remi had on a pair of blue jeans, a waist-length leather jacket and her favourite sneakers. Tenisha had on a long imitation leopardskin coat and large moon style boots with fur lining. Remi looked up from the book she had been reading and stared, disgusted, as she saw the white worm-like larvae that Darren held in his hands. She shivered slightly at the thought of them wriggling on her hand.

Tenisha, searching for something to do, stood up from her position next to her friend and picked up a stone. She threw it expertly into the pond, hoping to see it skip over the water, but unfortunately it sunk immediately, making a noisy plopping noise as it fell.

"Hey!" Tyrone shouted. "You'll scare the fish away."

Tenisha shrugged her shoulders in resignation and would have given him backchat had it not been for the sharp look that Darren gave her.

"All this business about Native Americans," Tyrone said, changing the subject, "I think it's the weirdest thing we've ever done at school."

"That's right," Tenisha said in agreement. "What I want to know is where is it going to get us?"

"And I've got to work with Georgina Wagstaff. I can't even get a word in edgeways with her."

The friends nodded their heads in sympathy. They could imagine just what Tyrone was going through. Georgina was one of those girls who thought she knew everything and had been everywhere. If a new film came out in the cinema, Georgina would boast that she had seen it ages before. Or if someone came in with the latest sneakers, Georgina would turn her nose in the air and say that she had a pair like that when she went on holiday. And if by chance there was something that you had that she wanted, you had better watch out because she would go out of her way to get it and start posing off in it, saying that she'd got it long before you.

"Luckily, my partner is much easier to

work with," Remi boasted.

Darren looked at Tyrone and rolled his eyes upwards.

"Junior is brilliant. He knows so much about everything," Remi continued. She blushed a little as she spoke and hoped that no one had noticed. She didn't want to give away the fact that she hoped Junior might one day be more than just a project partner. "Do you know," she continued coolly, "that he has a collection of honour feathers?"

"Honour feathers? What are those?" asked Tenisha.

"They were awarded by some Native American tribes for acts of bravery," replied Remi.

Darren kissed his teeth and turned to Tyrone. "Honour feathers won't do you much good when you're lying flat-out in the middle of Harvest Festival, will they?" he said.

Tyrone snorted in amusement. He might have questioned Darren's attitude towards Junior, but he remained loyal to his best friend, and Junior tripping over had been the best laugh in school for weeks.

"Mr Singh almost blew a blood vessel," Tenisha giggled.

Tyrone's eyes started to water as he remembered the strict teacher's fury at being covered in egg yolk. He wiped a small tear with the back of his hand. Darren's little prank had made the classes seem much less boring that day. It had been the topic of conversation for the whole of the lower school.

"Well, I think it was cruel of you, Darren," said Remi, coming to the defence of her new friend. "Junior might have been really hurt, falling like that with his hands full of Harvest Festival stuff. And what if one of the tins he was carrying had hit someone on the head?" A thought suddenly struck Remi as she spoke. "What if Mr Singh had been hit by a tin of baked beans instead of the eggs? What would you have done then?"

It was no use Remi considering how serious Darren's actions might have been when her three friends were rolling around on the river bank in uncontrollable fits of laughter at the memory of eggy Mr Singh. She couldn't keep a straight face any longer and finally burst into giggles herself. "Darren, I will never forget the look on Mr Singh's face," she blurted out. "It was brilliant."

And all four of them howled with painful laughter until tears were rolling down their cheeks.

It was a good fifteen minutes before they had all calmed down. The boys returned to their fishing while Tenisha continued reading her book. Remi, however, was not so relaxed. Although she had been laughing about Mr Singh, she was worried about the Harvest Festival — not about what happened in assembly, but about what *hadn't* happened in the afternoon.

"Darren?" she said at last.

"Yeah?" said Darren, absently.

"What happened with you and Junior after school on the day of Harvest Festival? Everyone thought there was going to be a fight, but when we got to the bike sheds you weren't there. Did you fight?"

"Yeah, we did," Darren said. "And I whopped his hide, okay?"

Remi glared at him and then at Tyrone. "Is that true? Were you there, Ty? Did you let it happen?"

"I couldn't stop them, Remi. Sorry. I did my best."

An uneasy silence fell over the four friends as they each stared out across the canal. Remi seethed in silent fury at the thought of what Darren had done to Junior; Darren sulked about the way Remi had spoken to him; Tyrone felt guilty about his failure to keep Darren and Junior apart; and Tenisha just wished someone would say something.

In the end, it was Darren who broke the silence. "Imagine," he said, turning to the girls, "having a bug for a pet." Darren held one of the maggots between his thumb and forefinger.

"Eurrgh!" Tenisha spluttered, grabbing her throat and making retching noises. "A bug as a pet — how could you?"

"Yeah, and bugs don't do much," said

Tyrone. "A dog, now that's a pet."

Darren looked up, his face beaming. He had succeeded in making an impression on his friends as he always loved to do.

"Yes, but what you don't realise," he said, raising his voice slightly, "is that there's never a dull moment with bugs."

Tenisha frowned from behind her spectacles.

"You can always tell it to bug off if it gets on your nerves," said Darren, grinning broadly.

Tyrone laughed out loud. "That's just what I feel like doing to Georgina."

Remi closed her book and placed it beside her on the grass. Darren saw it there and couldn't resist walking over and picking it up.

"Also," he added with a glint in his eye, "bugs make great bookmarks." He dangled one of the maggots tauntingly above the open pages of the hardback book. Then, without warning, he snapped the book shut.

Each one of his three friends cried out in horror. "Euuuurrgh! Nasty." "That's so cruel." "Man, you're dark... seriously dark."

"That's really horrible," Tenisha said, before she realised that Darren hadn't really squashed the maggot into the pages of Remi's book.

Darren, a cheeky grin spread across his face, waved the wriggling maggot in front of Remi and hopped from one foot to the other in a kind of victory dance borrowed from an Apache in a western he had recently seen on TV.

"Yeah, imagine if you died and you came back as a worm or something," Tenisha said, removing her steamed-up spectacles.

"Do you mean reincarnation?" Darren enquired, sitting down on the grass again.

Tenisha nodded as she cleaned the lenses on her sleeve.

"Nah!" Darren said emphatically. "When you die that's it... Here lies Joe Bloggs, he's dead, that's it."

A sudden sense of sadness gripped the four friends. For a minute or so they sat in silence, each person lost in his or her own thoughts. Nobody moved.

Darren was the first to speak. Staring at the motionless fishing rod floats in the water, he shook his head and said, "I don't think the fish are going to bite today."

The weekend had been so enjoyable that by Monday morning Darren had forgotten about his punishment at school. He was in the changing room getting ready for PE when Mr Adams came up to him with a pair of rubber gloves and a metal wastepaper basket.

"Here, James, I think these belong to you."

"No, sir, I'm sure that they don't." Darren wondered what had possessed his teacher to come out with such a thing.

"Oh, yes they do," Mr Adams said, nodding. "You are going to take these and pick up all the litter in the playground."

It was then that Darren remembered. "But sir...!"

But it was no use. Mr Adams was having none of it. He had no time for sob stories or excuses and simply dropped the gloves and basket at Darren's feet. "I'm sorry James, but rules are rules," he said.

An argument was developing at the far end of the changing room and the teacher moved his burly frame swiftly to investigate.

Darren wished that the floor would open up and swallow him up or that lightning would strike him in the chest. That would be a better fate for him than what he'd been asked to do. Reluctantly, head bowed and seething, he snatched the gloves off the floor and aimed a kick at the bin which made a clanging noise as it rolled towards the door.

The playground was littered with the debris of a typical day at Drummond Hill Comprehensive, which is to say it was covered in sweet wrappers, empty crisps bags, ice lolly sticks and the odd abandoned training shoe. Darren had only been on litter duty a couple of minutes before he heard the first cat calls from a pupil hanging out of a window on the first floor of the school building.

"You missed a bit," said the boy, throwing a rolled up piece of paper through the air. It landed a few feet from where Darren was standing. Darren was just about to fling the paper ball back in the boy's face when he caught sight of Mr Fredericks, standing at his office window checking on his progress. Darren had no choice but to pick it up in his gloved hand.

I hope this won't happen all week, Darren thought to himself. He made a show of picking up the litter, all the while moving towards the bike sheds, knowing that once he reached them he would be away from the prying eyes of the Head and the other pupils.

When he got there, he crouched down and wrapped his arms around himself. He felt safe. He and Tyrone used to come here when they were in Year 7 to trade football stickers. He remembered how when the bell would ring for break-time all the rest of the kids would race out towards the basketball courts or walk aimlessly across the playground. Darren and Tyrone didn't care for such things at the time. They would take out their cards and separate them into packs and fan them out for a better view. Then they would begin swapping. There were rules for the trading. Alan Shearer was worth two Diego Maradonnas, a rare Les Ferdinand in his old QPR kit was worth almost any number of cards that you could mention. Tyrone's cards were always the most impressive because his would have that looked-at-a-lot, frayed-at-the-edges feel to them, whereas Darren's were always quite new, on account of the fact that he received a lot more pocket money and could buy them more often. This usually meant that he completed his set before Tyrone was even half-way through.

Yes, behind the bike shed was always the place where Darren could find sanctuary. He stayed there for the rest of the morning. When the bell rang for lunch, he made his way back into the school with a half-full bin in his hand. He had just pushed open the double swing doors when Patrick Annette came running up to him.

"Hey, Darren," he said, waving, "I think you're for the high jump." And he gave him a sickly smirk.

"Why's that?"

"The Head wants you in his office."

Darren's heart missed a beat. The thought crossed his mind that he had been rumbled, but he couldn't figure out how the Head could have seen him skiving.

It was only a short walk from the swing doors to Mr Fredericks's office, but it seemed to Darren that it had to be the longest he had taken in his life. When he finally stood outside the office he almost turned away at the sound of Mr Fredericks mumbling away to himself inside. Darren's hand wavered before he rapped his knuckles lightly on the door. Mr Fredericks couldn't have heard so he knocked again, this time a little louder.

"Come in," ordered the headmaster from the other side of the door.

Darren opened the door cautiously, avoiding Mr Fredericks's stare as he stepped into the large study. All that he could think of as the headmaster grumbled "Hrumph!" was whether or not he was going to be expelled.

The headmaster was seated on his large

brown leather sofa and didn't look up at Darren. Instead he was shuffling some papers that were on his table. Darren shifted uneasily. He wanted to make like an atom and split, but his legs were unable to move.

After what seemed like an eternity the Head finally spoke.

"I was watching you out in the playground earlier."

Oh-oh! thought Darren. Now I'm for it.

"And I must say you seemed to be doing a good job."

It took Darren a few seconds to figure out what the headmaster was saying. At first he thought he was hearing things, but when he dared to look into the Head's face it didn't seem be angry, so Darren remained silent. This time he could make out clearly what was being said to him.

"I am extremely worried about you, Darren James. You are a boy who seems never to be out of trouble. However, I do not want to punish you for the sake of it. You should have learnt your lesson in the art of honesty."

Darren nodded and stared over Mr Fredericks's shoulder, out of the window into the playground that was already filling up with pupils. Then he directed his gaze back to the headmaster, putting on his saddest face. It was one that he had been practising in front of the bathroom mirror for days.

"Honesty, Darren James — that is the key word. Do you understand?"

Darren nodded. Honesty was the same word his father had used the other night when he had been sounding off at him.

"Judging by the look on your face, I think that you've learnt an important lesson, and I believe in rewarding those who learn carefully. Consequently, I'm prepared to give you another chance," Mr Fredericks continued.

When the headmaster finally dismissed him from the office Darren almost jumped for joy. He could not believe his luck. Not only had he escaped the curse of picking up rubbish, but the Head felt he had done such a good job that he was letting him off from doing any more. He decided that he could really get to like school if things carried on like this.

CHAPTER TEN

Remi had asked Junior to come to her house so that they could finish off their project. He turned up in all the latest garms, looking well cool. He said that he had bought them earlier.

Wow! Remi thought to herself. He must be well rich. She should have guessed that all was not going according to plan when her mother started fussing over him as soon as he walked through the door.

"Would you like a soft drink?" she asked him as he walked into the kitchen. The kitchen was the most popular room in the Oluseyi household. It was the room where messages to other members of the family were written and received. That was one of the house rules. Dad had rules at home just as he did at work.

Mum owned the only West Indian restaurant in the High Street. She made it so that the kitchen in the house was run like that in her restaurant — lively but homely, a place where you would go to eat, drink and socialise.

Remi peered over to where her mother stood, and she could see Junior from the corner of her eye grinning in that lopsided way of his at her mother.

Junior politely refused the drink. "I must say that is a lovely outfit you have on," he commented.

Mrs Oluseyi blushed as she smoothed down her sarong-style designer skirt. There weren't many of her daughter's friends that she approved of, but this boy seemed so nice and charming, and he dressed well.

Remi stood behind Junior, wishing that the floor would open up and swallow her. She cringed when she saw her mother rushing about all over the place like a headless chicken. The only time her mum went on like this was when Dad would come home from work with a bunch of flowers and a bottle of wine and blow suggestively in her ear. She could understand that — but Junior... ?

"Look, Mum," she said hurriedly, "we've got our project to finish off. We'll just head up to my room."

Mrs Oluseyi frowned, concerned. Allowing Remi to invite boys into her room was not something she did often, but Junior seemed such a nice person... She nodded and smoothed down her hair as the two school mates headed out of the door.

In Remi's room on the first floor, Junior made towards the mirror at the far end of the room. He stood in front of it and studied his reflection. Seemingly satisfied, he turned to face Remi. She should have guessed something was up because he seemed to be avoiding eye contact with her. That was weird because Remi was always being told that she had nice eyes. She figured that Junior was like the rest of the boys, embarrassed to be talking to a girl and all that.

"I thought Darren was going to have a cow when he saw us together," Remi exclaimed.

Junior shrugged, peering absent-mindedly over her shoulder at the wall. He shifted his position uncomfortably, and Remi guessed that he was feeling the bruises from his fight with Darren.

"Are you all right?" she asked. It was an innocent question, but Junior responded as if he'd been smacked in the mouth.

"Don't ask me that," he spat. "Don't ever ask me that."

Remi stared at the carpet, her mouth quivering as her eyes threatened to fill with tears. She'd only wanted to be kind, to show Junior that she was on his side after the fight with Darren. There was no need to be vicious. Why had he spoken to her like that?

Junior also stared at the carpet. Stupid, stupid, stupid, stupid, he thought to himself. How was Remi supposed to know that he was so tired of people checking he was okay, of people tiptoeing around him as if he was going to break any minute? That's what it was like with sickle cell anaemia, everyone cooing at you. But it wasn't Remi's fault.

"Look, I'm sorry, Remi," he said. "You just caught me off guard, okay?"

Remi shuffled uncomfortably. Junior's attitude was not what she had expected. She searched for something to say. "Wouldn't it be better if people thought of us as a couple?"

She hadn't meant it to come out like it did, and her mind raced as she searched for something else to say, but nothing came. The silence in the room was deafening. Remi would have screamed if Junior hadn't broken it.

"That's what I wanted to talk to you about."

Oh-oh! the girl thought to herself. This sounds kinda serious. "What's the matter?" she asked.

"Like, what we think being a couple is all about."

"I don't follow," said Remi. She feared

that the conversation was going in a direction she didn't want it to.

"Well, I know we have to work together on the project, but sometimes the way you go on makes me feel..." He looked over at Remi. She was close to tears, her eyes lowered.

"So you don't like working with me?" Remi said simply.

"Nah, it's not that," Junior began. "I'm making this sound much worse than it should be, aren't I?"

"Yes, I think so." Remi nodded.

From somewhere deep inside him Junior understood how Remi was feeling. He could imagine how she must hate him. If she turned around and whacked him on the head, he knew he would deserve it. Although Remi had never said it in so many words, Junior knew that she relished the comments that had been going around the school about the two of them, and the envious glances he had seen some of the girls in their year giving her. He figured that there was no easy way for him to tell her that he did not want them to be an item.

"What I'm trying to say is — we can be good friends, but we should also see other people... I'll always be here to listen."

Remi could not believe what she was hearing. Though he was right when he said that she thought the two of them could be an item, she didn't realise that she had been so obvious.

"Of course we can see other people," she said, regaining her composure. "It's not as if we *are* an item, is it?"

Junior breathed an audible sigh of relief and nodding his head in agreement. "Now that's settled, let's get on with the project."

Remi nodded her head too, but her mind was really racing now. While Junior was going on about how they were going to present their topic, she imagined how Junior must have been having a laugh at her expense since they had been paired up.

Remi leaned her elbow on the table tennis table. "It's kinda strange." She sighed heavily.

"What is?" Darren inquired as he looked at the girl in a strange way. He held the ping pong ball between his thumb and forefinger, and the bat in the other hand, ready to serve the ball to Tyrone, who was waiting, bat in hand, at the other side of the table.

"When sometimes you are talking away to someone and you say something that sounds kinda stupid and it sort of echoes in your head, and you have to say something quick to hide it."

Darren stopped midway through his service action and walked over to Remi. He wondered what she could mean. He knew that she often went on a mind trip to the twilight zone, but what she was saying now was well loopy.

Or perhaps not, he mused to himself. He'd been having serious doubts about her lately. She was forever talking under her breath so he couldn't hear. And always defending Junior.

"I don't think I've ever had that problem," said Tyrone.

Remi stood straighter before she shrugged her shoulders. "I don't know," she sighed. "It's just that when someone compliments your parents, there's nothing you can say."

Darren nodded in agreement.

"It's like a stun gun to the brain." She placed a forefinger to her head and cocked her middle finger as though she was firing a gun.

It was almost nine o'clock and the Youth Club was about to shut for the evening.

Tenisha removed her glasses and examined them closely before she cleaned them thoroughly on the sleeve of her jacket.

"He didn't even want to talk about the project," Remi said.

The girls headed out of the swing doors on to the street. Kids were milling around outside, sharing a final joke before they made their way home.

"Doesn't he have a girlfriend in his other school?"

"Unhh?"

"That's what I hear. I think you'd better hold your horses," Tenisha said.

"What do you mean?"

"What you were saying. I think that you were expecting too much."

Remi's brow was wrinkled. Tenisha took her friend by the arm. She quickly looked over her shoulder, taking care that Darren couldn't hear what she was about to say.

"Well, I've learnt some disturbing things about Junior... You were going on about Junior, weren't you?"

"Yeah, of course," Remi replied, lowering her voice. She didn't know why, but she too looked over to where Darren and Tyrone were standing.

"I know you think he is a nice boy," Tenisha began, "but do you realise that he dumps all his girlfriends because they won't snog him?" There, she had said it. She examined her friend's face. Remi paced to and fro while Tenisha hoped that her words were sinking in and that she would not have to say what else she knew about Junior.

Remi seemed hurt. She could feel her cheeks flushing. Tenisha often went on as though she was her good conscience. People would often joke that she was like her sensible older sister. It sounded to her that Tenisha was telling the truth, but the truth was not what she wanted to hear at this particular moment. Anyway, Junior had never asked her to snog him. The thought of Junior carrying on that way disgusted her.

"Are you okay?"

Remi seemed to have lost a lot of the colour in her face and was starting to look quite ill. She stopped her pacing as it was making her a little giddy. "Yes... yes," she stammered hurriedly. "I told you — me and Junior are just good friends."

"Mmm," Tenisha mumbled. She removed her spectacles and fingered the piece of tape that held the frames together with a practised touch before cleaning them rigorously again on the sleeve of her sweatshirt. "Georgina Wagstaff," she began. She emphasised the words so that Remi would realise where the gossip was coming from. "Georgina Wagstaff dared him to kiss her. So he did."

"If he wants to give tongue sandwiches to

Georgina Wagstaff that's up to him. Anyway, I'm glad I'm over it," Remi said.

"Remi?"

"What?"

"You're not over it."

"Oh, by the way," Remi said. "If Junior asks, we were out together last night on a double date."

"Who with?" Tenisha said.

Remi shrugged. She looked around at the group of boys leaning on the wall opposite. "What about Philip Hector?"

"No way," Tenisha replied determinedly, "he drools."

"Okay it was two other guys."

"What did they look like, what did they wear, what did we eat?" Tenisha asked.

"Tenisha."

"Yeah?"

"I'm gonna hit you."

CHAPTER ELEVEN

The following Monday morning, Darren cornered the PE teacher outside the gym. He couldn't understand everything that was going on. He had been feeling all tensed up in the shoulders since Junior had appeared on the scene. Mr Adams refused to give him back his position on the team on account that it would be difficult to leave Junior out of the squad, since his performance was so good.

"But sir," Darren complained, "I'm way better than the rest of them. Why can't I take someone else's place?"

"But that wouldn't be fair on all the others who actually turned up for practice."

"But sir, you know I couldn't."

"That's right," nodded Mr Adams. "You were under punishment, and that's no way for a captain to behave."

Darren knew it was hopeless to argue. How he hated Junior. It seemed to him that Junior was a fraud, and that no one else could see it apart from him. And if that wasn't bad enough, even Remi seemed to diss him. He could not make out the reason for her to blank him whenever their paths crossed in school. And the only things she talked about when she decided to give him a moment of her time were her Native American project or how Junior was saying this or saying that. As if Darren wanted to know about his weak attempts at cracking a joke. And on top of all that, everyone was going on about a couple of lucky points Junior had scored at the basketball game. As far as Darren was concerned, that didn't count for much. If he had been chosen, the match would have been over very quickly.

"Anyway," Darren said to himself. "It's not as if we've won anything — there's still the final to play. He decided then that the final was when he would reclaim his rightful place on the team.

Boy, how he hated Junior! He hated him for making him feel so upset with Remi. He realised that she had to do what she felt like doing; it wasn't like he owned her. It was up to her if she had decided that she didn't want to telephone him any longer.

By the time he ambled into The Toupee's class, Darren was feeling totally fed up. The class were settling down at their tables when Junior, who was seated near the front, fell on the floor and started writhing about. He screamed so much that no one knew quite what was going on, and the way that he held on to his stomach frightened Darren. He imagined that he might have caused Junior some internal injuries when he had beaten him up the other day.

Junior was in terrible pain. He had his eyes shut tight. He knew not to panic and, holding back the tears, he concentrated on staying calm and trying to block out the agony he was feeling. Even so, he couldn't help but wonder, Is this the end? as his body tensed. From somewhere far away he could hear the voices of his classmates. "Give him some room," some of them said. "I bet he's on drugs," said a few others, just like they had at his last school.

Junior felt another flash of searing pain shoot through his body.

From his seat by the door, Tyrone saw everything. Within seconds he was kneeling beside Junior.

"Junior, are you okay?" he asked as he rested his classmate's head on his lap.

Junior's eyes were still shut tight, but he heard The Toupee telling someone to go to the headmaster's office.

"I think he's hurt bad," Tyrone shouted. "The Head won't do. Someone phone for an ambulance!"

Junior tried to get up but the pain was unbearable; he couldn't move.

Realising that he had to do something and despite the remonstrations of his teacher,

Tyrone indicated for Darren to come over. Together they lifted Junior into their arms and started running towards the matron's office on the first-floor landing. As they ran, Junior tried to speak, but his lips felt as though they were glued together.

"Just keep calm," said Tyrone through his own tears of panic. "You're safe with us."

By the time that Tyrone and Darren had got Junior to the matron's office, Junior had started to feel a little better. As he lay there nervously waiting for the ambulance to arrive, he held Tyrone's hand tight, certain that as long as Tyrone was around he was going to be okay.

So it was that Tyrone went to the hospital in the ambulance with Junior — he sensed that the sick boy needed him.

Later, when Junior was laid in a bed on one of the hospital wards, Tyrone heaved slightly when he saw the blood trickle slowly down one of the tubes into the needle that was stuck into Junior's arm with some tape. He felt uneasy as he stood there while Junior lay quite still and very quiet. He knew he must be in a bad way because it was not like Junior to keep quiet for so long.

"He wasn't even mad at you," Tyrone said incredulously as he and Darren walked to school the next morning.

"Maybe he's saving it for the police," Darren replied in a shaky voice. He hadn't slept well because he was worried he was responsible for Junior's illness.

"No," Tyrone said determinedly, "he's really sick. You've got to come and see him in hospital."

"But what's wrong with him, Ty? Was it my fault he got sick? Was it the fight?"

"I don't know, Darren. A lot of people are saying that maybe he was on drugs and that's what caused it. Whatever, will you come to the hospital?"

Darren didn't answer. He wasn't sure whether it would be right for him to visit Junior after all that had gone on.

At assembly that morning Mr Fredericks made a special announcement. There was a deathly quiet in the hall as his face twisted in anger.

"It has come to my notice that there has been a lot of false talk concerning one of the pupils in the school." His cheeks puffed out as he spoke. Even from where Darren was sitting near the back of the hall, he could tell that the headmaster was furious. He knew what the talk had been about since Junior had been taken ill. Like Tyrone had said, everyone was going on about how Junior could be on drugs.

"That sort of talk is intolerable," continued Mr Fredericks as he fought hard to control the anger that was rising inside him. "That is why there has been a special talk prepared for you."

He stepped down from the platform and left the whole of the lower school seated. A smartly dressed man in a blue pin-striped suit replaced the headmaster on the stage. He cleared his throat before he spoke.

"Hi! My name is Ade Alekhine," he said,

waving his hand. "My task this morning is to tell you about an illness which one of your friends is suffering from. After I have finished I am sure that some of you will have questions you want to ask, which I will be glad to answer."

Mr Alekhine went on to tell them about how some diseases can be passed from parents to children in their genes, and how some of these genetic diseases affect people from one race more than others.

"One such inherited blood disorder is sickle cell anaemia," he said as he looked up at the rapt audience. He explained that it occurs mainly in members of the African race. "That includes those of you who have parents from the Caribbean," he said, as though reading the minds of some of the kids who had mothers and fathers that came from Jamaica, Barbados and the other islands. He explained that the gene has to be present in both parents to be inherited by their offspring.

"Persons that inherit the sickling gene from only one parent do not get the disease," emphasised Mr Alekhine. "But they can transmit the abnormal gene to their children."

Someone from the back of the hall put up their hand.

"Yes, what is it?"

"Sir," said the confused boy, "why do people have it in the first place?"

"I'm glad you asked that question," the man said with a grin. "If it was not for the fact that our ancestors had the defective gene, most of us would not be here today."

The boy's face was still screwed up in a frown as he tried to figure out what he was being told. "I don't understand what you mean, sir," he said finally.

Mr Alekhine went on to explain that genetic carriers of sickle cell anaemia are relatively immune to malaria, and that they hardly ever get ill after they are bitten by a malaria carrying mosquito. He told them that the abnormal gene has come to be an advantage in some areas of the Caribbean, Africa and southern Europe where malaria is a life threatening disease.

"This is an example of how the genetic make-up of races changes to meet the pressures of the environment," said Mr Alekhine as he finished his talk.

He took a cursory look around the room. "Are there any questions?"

Darren's hand shot up. "So what you're saying is that Africans and Caribbeans have a hard time of it?"

Mr Alekhine nodded his head slowly before he replied. "Yes, but what I'm also saying is that hereditary disease is not unique to people of that racial grouping. For example, PKU, a disease that hinders amino acid transfer in the body, occurs among the European geographical race more often than other groups."

"What is the effect of PKU?"

"Unless treated early it results in mental retardation. Any other questions?"

The discussion continued a while longer until he dismissed the lower school.

It was almost six o'clock when they arrived

at the hospital. Junior was just as Tyrone had left him the day before. Darren made to turn his head away, but instead he found himself staring open-mouthed at what he saw. There was a machine to one side of the bed which made a bleeping noise.

Junior's eyes flickered open. Tyrone nudged Darren in the ribs.

"Go on, say something."

"Respect," Darren said, offering a fist to Junior as he lay quite still.

Tyrone cringed from where he stood. It seemed to him that Darren was taking everything as a joke. The least he could do was seem a little concerned, even if he didn't mean it. He exchanged looks with Darren when Junior didn't move. Darren shrugged his shoulders.

The silence was interrupted at short intervals by the machine as the two boys waited for Junior to speak. The hands on the clock above the door moved silently around. Next to it was a large red sign with a "No Smoking" warning. Tyrone smiled wryly when he saw it. He wondered who would be silly enough to start puffing away when people were lying down hardly able to breathe. The rest of the room was sparsely furnished with three chairs and a bedside table with a bowl of fruit and some get-well cards on it.

Tyrone mumbled that he'd brought something. He pulled out a Lucozade bottle from the carrier bag that he had with him. As he placed the bottle next to the fruit, he happened to glance at some of the cards. One was from somebody called Michelle and it had loads of kisses on it. Tyrone didn't remember a Michelle in their year. He did, however, recognise a card signed by some his friends at school. He saw his own spider-like signature with the little smiley figure he had drawn by it. Somehow he knew that Junior would have enjoyed that little touch. He swivelled around when he heard Junior make a little groan from where he lay.

"What you sayin'?" Junior said in such a low voice that Tyrone had to lean forward to catch it. His eyes shifted to Darren, who tried his best to avoid Junior's gaze.

"We brought you something to drink," said Tyrone.

"Thanks," Junior whispered weakly. He winked at Darren who nodded back.

"Haven't you got the match tomorrow?" Junior continued.

"Yeah, that's right. I guess I should thank you for getting sick just in time for me to be made captain of the team again."

Tyrone frowned at Darren.

"But I don't really feel like that," Darren added. "Still, I'm going to make the opposition well dizzy!" he exclaimed. Then, seeing the downcast look on Junior's face, he added, "I just wish we could both be playing."

"Yeah."

Junior looked past Darren's head when he heard the door opening. Darren and Tyrone turned and saw Remi with a bunch of flowers in her hand.

"I guess we'll have to go now," Tyrone said, tugging at his friend's arm.

Darren agreed and both boys were making

their way out of the room when they heard Junior calling out in a weak voice.

Darren turned his head slightly. "What's up?" he asked.

"No hard feelings, man. Score a couple of points for me."

Darren suddenly felt guilty as he remembered how he had treated Junior since he'd started at the school. He hated the way that he had thought Junior was just bigging up himself and was trying to take his friends away from him. He knew now it hadn't really been his fault; he was just trying to deal with always getting ill.

"You know, Junior, you're safe," Darren said, holding up a fist.

Junior nodded his head and watched as the door swung shut behind them.

When they had closed the door, Junior turned to Remi.

"Hi, how are you?" he whispered.

"Fine. Better than you look, I expect."

"Thanks for the observation," said Junior, smiling.

Remi pulled a bag of grapes out of her bag

and set them in the fruit bowl. She spied Michelle's card. Turning, she reached into her bag again and smiled as she pulled out a couple of gymnastics magazines.

Junior grinned weakly. "That's what I like about you," he said, "you're a girl that's got a mind of her own."

"Yeah, and I want to know why you never told us about your sickle cell anaemia."

Junior smiled wryly. "I thought you'd all feel sorry for me if you knew I was ill," he said. "In some stupid way, I thought everyone would actually like big, tough Junior."

"Don't be silly," Remi chided. "The only way to be liked is to be yourself."

"I think I've got that message." Junior smiled again. "Look, Remi. Will you do me a favour? Tell Darren to play a wicked game for me."

Remi nodded.

CHAPTER TWELVE

The cheering around the court was almost deafening. The gymnasium at Drummond Hill had been converted so that spectators could see the match easily. The hall was packed with pupils. Mr Fredericks sat at the side of the court on a bench, wringing his hands expectantly. Remi and Tenisha sat a few places along. They waved small flags in the school colours above their heads in unison with the rest of the pupils. Anton stood at the other end of the court by the scoreboard, having been appointed the official scoremaster. Not surprisingly, he hadn't managed to get into the team, but it seemed that all the hours of pain he had gone through, and the endless extra laps that Mr Adams had heaped on him, had paid off. Mr Adams had recognised his commitment and given him this important job. He stood proudly, score cards in hand, waiting for the match to begin.

Darren's parents stood a few rows back. Lester was holding court with some of the other dads, telling them of his plans to surprise Darren with the rest of the money for that leather jacket he knew his son had his eye on. Yvonne was chatting excitedly with Tyrone's mum, Marcia, somewhere in the crowd. Patricia waved and cheered with her posse, a bevy of admirers surrounding her. The atmosphere was electric.

Remi turned and placed a hand on Tenisha's. "I just know that Darren is going to play a wicked game."

Suddenly the crowd cheered loudly in anticipation as the two teams were announced.

"So what, did you make it up with Junior at the hospital?" Tenisha said, removing her spectacles.

Remi looked at her strangely before she spoke. "Why do you think we ever had anything going?"

Tenisha shrugged her shoulders. She looked at her spectacles intently before cleaning them on her sleeve and placing them back on the bridge of her nose.

Her eyes lit up as she focused through her glasses on the two teams running on to the court. They stood in the middle and turned to face the crowd. Tenisha stood up and cheered along with everyone else, her flag fluttering from side to side as she waved it frantically. From behind her a group of pupils were chanting away: "Two, four, six, eight, who do we appreciate..." Tenisha sat down as the chanting was taken up by everyone. "DRUMMOND!"

Darren played a terrific game. His experiences of the last few days and the fact that he had very nearly failed to make the team had filled him with renewed energy and determination. Fortunately for his team, their passes to him invariably resulted in the ball sailing through the opposition's basket, and even the odd loose ball was swiftly intercepted by him and turned to their advantage. The other team didn't stand a chance.

At the match's victorious end, everyone agreed that Darren should be nominated as the man of the match. He climbed the steps to where the mayor was standing with the cup in hand.

Tyrone, who was behind him, nudged him in the ribs.

"Look over there!"

Leaning on a pair of crutches was Junior, supported on one side by a girl, who they presumed to be Michelle.

"Hey, Junior, come over here," Darren waved.

The crowd fell silent as they watched the boy helped on to the stage.

"I think you should lift the cup. After all, if it hadn't been for you we would never have reached the final."

Junior grinned weakly. "I don't think I can

MY MUM WENT BALLISTIC ABOUT MY REPORT FROM LAST TERM... AND IF MY GRADES DON'T GET BETTER, SHE'S GONNA SEND ME TO LIVE WITH MY UNCLE CHARLES IN SCOTLAND!!
YOU MEAN THAT ONE THAT THINKS HE'S IN THE ARMY? BWOY, I DON'T ENVY YOU THERE!
ANYWAY, HERE COME REMI AND TENISHA NOW. NOT A WORD, YEAH?
COOL, DARREN. ANYWAY, I'VE GOTTA DUCK OUT NOW. I'VE HAD COMPUTER TIME BOOKED SINCE LAST TERM, AND I'M ALREADY LATE! CATCH YA LATER!!
HI, DARREN. LIKE MY NEW JACKET? MY DAD GOT IT FOR ME FOR GETTING...
..TOP GRADES IN HER CLASS!!
HI REMI, TENISHA. THAT'S ALL GOOD, BUT THE ONLY THING MY PARENTS HAVE FOR ME IS THE BELT!
ANYWAY, I'VE GOT MORE IMPORTANT THINGS TO WORRY 'BOUT THAN NEW CLOTHES! LISTEN, REMI! I'M OUT!!
WHATS WRONG WITH DARREN, REMI?
I DUNNO, TENISHA. HE MIGHT BE MY MAN, BUT SOMETIMES HE'S A MYSTERY TO ME...
THEN...
WELL, IF IT AIN'T SWEET BWOY DARREN JAMES!
LEAVE IT, MARVIN. I'M NOT IN THE MOOD.
HEAR THAT, MARY? POOR DARREN'S UPSET! AAAH!!
YOU SHOULD'VE JOINED THE SMOKERS CORNER CREW FROM TIME, MAN! WE NEVER HAVE ANY WORRIES, MY YOUT! LISTEN, YOU WANT SOME OF THIS?
TH-THATS A FAG, INNIT?
FAG, SALMON, CIGGIE... WHATEVER YOU CALL IT, IT'S SURE TO MAKE ALL YOUR WORRIES JUST FLOAT AWAY!!
UM... OKAY... BUT JUST ONE PULL, ALRIGHT?
FFFTT
MY MUM'D KILL ME IF SHE SAW ME DOING THIS! BUT...
DARREN JAMES... WELCOME TO THE SMOKER'S CORNER CREW!!
YEAH!!

LATER...
NOW, TO RECAP ON THE LAST...
SLAM!!
PUFF, PUFF!
WHAT THE -- DARREN JAMES?
WHAT KIND OF TIME IS THIS TO ENTER MY CLASS, JAMES?
LOOK AT THAT TOUPEE!
SORRY I'M LATE, SIR.
WHATS SO FUNNY, JAMES? AND WHAT'S THAT EXPRESSION ON YOUR FACE??
DONT KNOW SIR.
OH, JUST GO AND TAKE YOUR SEAT!
AND NO SCRAPING YOUR CHAIR ON THE FLOOR!
NO, SIR.
SNIGGER
PSST! DARREN! WHAT WAS THAT ABOUT? AND HOW COME YOU'RE SO LATE, MAN?
COOL, TYRONE. EVERYTHINGS ALRIGHT NOW...
BUT YOU WERE SO DOWN EARLIER, AND NOW YOU'RE.. WELL NOT HAPPY, BUT...
SNIGGER
SPURS
AHEM WHEN TYRONE AND DARREN HAVE STOPPED JABBERING ON, EXPLAIN THE WATER CYCLE....

...DARREN!!
ME? OH.. THE WATER CYCLE BEGINS WHEN YOU DRINK SOME WATER FROM THE TAP..
..AND AFTER A FEW HOURS, YOU GO TO THE TOILET AND PI
DARREN! OUT OF MY CLASS NOW!!
LUNCHTIME...
DID YA SEE DARREN IN SCIENCE TODAY? HE LOOKED MASH-UP!
YEAH, I DUNNO WHAT'S UP WITH HIM TODAY, TENISHA...
HE DIDN'T EVEN WANT TO TALK TO ME EARLIER...
WELL, REMI. IF HE WAS MY MAN, HE'D HAVE TO FIX UP!!
WHAT MAN? OH, YOU MUST MEAN OUR OWN EATING MACHINE..
..ANTON! WHA! YA SAYIN', HOMES?
CRUNCH, MUNCH!
I'M ALRIGHT, TYRONE. LISTEN, I JUST SAW DARREN GETTING AN EAR-FUL FROM THE TOUPÉE!
YEAH, HE STARTED ACTING ALL WEIRD IN CLASS EARLIER..
WHAT? HIS FIRST DAY BACK, WITH HIS RECORD? PUSHING IT A BIT, AIN'T HE?
YEAH, WELL YOU KNOW WHAT HE'S LIKE!
I COULD USE MY E.S.P AND TRY TO WORK OUT WHATS WRONG!
CHEW!
YOU AND YOUR E.S.P THIS AND TAROT CARD THAT, TEN!!
YOU COULDN'T READ THE BACK OF A CORNFLAKES BOX, LET ALONE SOME-ONE'S PALM!!
YES I COULD! I HAVE MYSTICAL POWERS!
OH, YEAH? WELL, TELL US WHEN ANTONS BABY IS DUE, THEN.
WHAT?
WELL, YOU'VE GOTTA ADMIT... HE IS EATING FOR TWO!!
HA, HA, HA, HA, HA!

AFTER LUNCH, DARREN AND TYRONE HAVE A P.E CLASS ... BASKETBALL!!
SO, DARREN, YOU FEEL BETTER NOW? WHAT DID OLD TOUPEE SAY TO YOU?
OH, YOU KNOW, THE USUAL: 'YOU MUST DO BETTER, DARREN!' BLAH, BLAH, BLAH!
EXIT
ANYWAY, LETS PLAY B-BALL, ALRIGHT?
THINK YOU CAN GET PAST ME, JAY?
ANYTIME, DAZ-MAN, ANYTIME!
BLOCK HIM DARREN!
THEN...
HA, HA, HA! DALLIED!!
OH!! NUTMEGGED! HA, HA, HAA!!
WHAM!
RIGHT, JAMES! MY OFFICE! NOW!!
DON'T WORRY! I'M OUT OF HERE!
JEEZ, DARREN! WHATS WRONG WITH YOU??
LISTEN. NONE OF THEM CARE ABOUT ME, SO WHY SHOULD I CARE ABOUT THEM?
ALRIGHT, DARREN. I'LL TALK TO OUR HEAD OF YEAR. SEE IF SHE CAN DO ANYTHING, SEEN?

LATER, AFTER SCHOOL...
I TOLD OUR YEARHEAD ABOUT YOUR MUM, UNCLE AND SCOTLAND AND SHES SORTED EVERYONE OUT. THERES ONE SMALL THING THOUGH, DARREN...
206
THANKS, TYRONE. HANG ON! WHAT DO YOU MEAN 'ONE SMALL THING'??
THE SCIENCE REPORT FOR THE TOUPEE.. THE ONE FOR OVER THE HOLIDAYS? WELL, YOU'VE GOT TO HAND IT IN!!
THE ONE I WAS SUPPOSED TO DO, BUT ENDED UP ON THE PLAYSTATION INSTEAD?
YEAH! SO COME BY MY YARD AND USE THE COMPUTER I GOT FOR CHRISTMAS TO DO IT!
CAN I COME AND DO MINE TOO, TYRONE?
NO!!
JUST LOOK AT MY ESSAY TO GET AN IDEA, THEN LOAD IN YOUR DISK AND AWAY YOU GO!
GUNNERS
WRIGHTY
I'M GONNA GET US SOME MUNCHIES!
ALRIGHT, TY. THANKS.
GOD, I'LL NEVER BE ABLE TO DO ALL THIS... I CAN'T EVEN WORK THE COMPUTER GOOD LIKE TYRONE... UNLESS I...
DISK 1 TYRONE
COPY TO
DISK 2 DARREN
PRESS A TO COPY & PRINT
IBM
I'LL COPY TYRONES AND CHANGE IT UP A BIT LATER!
SOON...
GOTTA GO NOW, TY. MY MUMS EXPECTING ME BEFORE SIX. RESPECT, OKAY.
YEAH, ANYTIME, DARREN. WAITAMINUTE! WHAT JUST DROPPED OUT OF YOUR POCKET?

JEEZ, DARREN! IT'S A FAG!! IS THIS WHY YOU'VE BEEN CRAZY ALLDAY?
WELL, MY PROBLEMS WERE GETTING TO ME, AND MARVIN SAID..
MARVIN? DON'T YOU REMEMBER THE TROUBLE THE SMOKERS CORNER CREW CAUSED YOU LAST TERM? DARREN... THIS AIN'T THE ANSWER!
REMEMBER MY COUSIN JEFF? HE STARTED SMOKING..., AND WHERE IS HE NOW? JAIL, DOING ONE YEAR FOR ROBBING TO BUY FAGS! AND THATS WHERE THEY ALL END UP EVENTUALLY, MAN!
YEAH, TYRONE. YOU'RE RIGHT. I'LL DASH IT AWAY ON MY WAY HOME. LATERS, TY.
AT SCHOOL...
SO, DARREN. YOU READY FOR THE TOUPEE THIS MORNING?
YEAH, TYRONE. I'VE GOT A GOOD FEELING ABOUT TODAY!
IM GLAD TO SAY YOU ALL SCORED VERY HIGH ON YOUR ESSAYS.. OUTSTANDING MARKS..
BUT TYRONE, COULD I SEE YOU FOR A MOMENT, PLEASE...
IT LOOKS TO ME, FROM THE LANGUAGE AND STYLE, THAT YOU HAVE COPIED YOUR ESSAY FROM DARRENS!! WHAT DO YOU SAY TO THAT?
B-BUT I DIDN'T, SIR!
ERM.. SIR.. IT WASN'T TYRONE WHO DID THE COPYING.. IT WAS ME.. I WAS SO BEHIND, AND I KNEW THAT IF I DIDN'T GET A GOOD GRADE ON THIS ESSAY YOU'D HAVE TO WRITE TO MY MUM...
.. AND THEN MY MUM WOULD SEND ME TO SCOTLAND TO MY UNCLE.. SO DONT BLAME TYRONE, BLAME ME...

I'D GUESSED AS MUCH, DARREN. I JUST WANTED YOU TO COME CLEAN ABOUT IT.
SO, WHAT NOW, SIR?
I'LL GIVE YOU A CHANCE. SIT THIS TEST, AND I'LL TRANSFER THE RESULT TO YOUR ESSAY GRADE. FAIR ENOUGH?
HOW D'YOU THINK YOU DID, DARREN?
I DUNNO, TY. FINGERS CROSSED!
SOON...
WELL, DARREN... I'M PLEASED TO SAY YOU'VE GOT YOURSELF A B+! WELL DONE!!
YEESSS!!
AFTER SCHOOL...
SO, DARREN. IT WASN'T SO HARD WAS IT?
THAT'S OKAY FOR YOU TO SAY! YOU'RE BETTER AT LESSONS THAN ME!
NAH, MAN! IT JUST TAKES A BIT OF HARD WORK!
THERE'S ONE THING I'M BETTER THAN YOU AT THOUGH...
...BASKETBALL! HA, HA, HA!!

The X Press invites you to join the

DRUMMOND HILL CREW

Book Club

Write to us about the books you enjoyed and tell us about your favourite characters.

Keep updated with the news from Drummond Hill by sending your name and address to:

The Drummond Hill Crew Book Club
The X Press
6 Hoxton Square
London N1 6NU
Tel: 0171 729 1199

The **DRUMMOND HILL CREW** Series

LIVIN' LARGE

New boy Junior Brown arrives at Drummond Hill School dressed in the latest designer clothes and with enough money to buy all the friends he'll ever need. Junior quickly becomes the most popular boy in his year, but makes an enemy of Darren James when Remi, Darren's girl, takes an interest in the new boy. What's more, Junior has replaced him in the school basketball team. To Darren, Junior is acting too big for his boots and is a show-off, so he decides to investigate. If he can find out where the new boy is getting all his money from, he'll be able to expose him as bogus and get back his popularity, his place in the basketball team and his girl. But Junior isn't what he seems and Darren ends up discovering more than he bargained for.

ISBN 1-874509-34-4

AVAILABLE FROM WH SMITH AND ALL GOOD BOOKSHOPS

The DRUMMOND HILL CREW Series

AGE AIN'T NOTHING BUT A NUMBER

When some of the pupils from Drummond Hill go on a school trip to the mysterious Headstone Manor, they find themselves right in the middle of an adventure! Are the strange noises in the night really made by a ghost?

ISBN 1-874509-33-6

AVAILABLE FROM WH SMITH AND ALL GOOD BOOKSHOPS

A WHOLE NEW SET OF DRUMMOND HILL CREW BOOKS WILL BE AVAILABLE IN THE SUMMER

DON'T MISS OUT ON MORE HILARIOUS ANTICS WITH DARREN, TYRONE, REMI, TENISHA AND ANTON.